AIRSHIP 27 PRODUCTIONS

Published by Airship 27 Productions
www.airship27.com
www.airship27hangar.com



Editor: Ron Fortier
Associate Editor: Charles Saunders
Marketing and Promotions Manager: Michael Vance
Production and design by Rob Davis.



ISBN-13: 978-0692611791 (Airship 27)
ISBN-10: 0692611797

Printed in the United States of America

10 9 8 7 6 5 4 3 2 1

# BASS REEVES FRONTIER MARSHAL

## CONTENTS:

# INTRODUCTION

by Ron Fortier

The old time-worn adage tells us that the truth is always stranger than fiction. Wish I had a dollar for every time that has been borne out in my own life. History is jam-packed with stories that if Hollywood were to come along and develop them nobody would ever believe they were based on fact. But as is often the case, the most amazing tales are the ones that actually happened.

Such as the life of U.S. Deputy Marshal Bass Reeves; a former slave who ran away from the Texas ranch he was living on to live with Indians in the Oklahoma territories that made up the Five Civilized Tribes. After the Civil War, Reeves married, built his own horse ranch and started raising a very large family. By the time the famous Judge Parker arrived in Fort Smith to establish a federal circuit court, he soon realized he had a major problem; his white marshals were unable to operate in remote townships settled by freed blacks, native Americans or established as outlaw sanctuaries. In the end the only solution was to deputize black men; one of the first of these being Bass Reeves.

During his thirty odd year career as a marshal, Reeves brought in over 3,000 felons even though he was illiterate and couldn't even read the writs he handed out. Due to his time with the Indian tribes, he was a skilled hunter-tracker, familiar with the territory and an expert in firearms, both pistols and rifles. He also learned to disguise himself as a vagabond when needing to infiltrate an outlaw camp and find his man. He was in fourteen major gun battles but never wounded once.

In the end, Reeves even hunted down his eldest son who had, in a moment of rage, shot his wife upon finding her with another man. None of the other marshals, in deference to Reeves, would accept the writ. When Reeves learned of the crime, he requested it and rode out to bring in his son. Young Reeves was convicted and sentenced to a life in the Yuma Federal Prison. Reeves retired shortly thereafter, the incident having been the one sour note to an otherwise amazing, and proud career as a lawman. After his death at the age of 70, friends and public officials petitioned the Arizona governor and his son's sentence was commuted.

Obviously I've just given you an encapsulated biography. Being a student of history, you can imagine my total surprise when I eventually learned of Reeves' existence. How was it possible I could have gone so long in my life without ever having heard of this man? The answer is simple, Bass Reeves' accomplishments were swept under the rug of history by prejudicial white teachers who purposely chose to ignore the contributions of blacks in the settling of the western frontier. It has only been in the last few decades that scholars such as Prof. Art Burton and others have delivered well researched biographies on Reeves and other black cowboys. Thus today, at long last, these remarkable stories are coming to light.

What follows are four fictional adventures by a quartet of western fans who jumped at the chance to write about Bass Reeves. We hope you'll enjoy them and they will spur (pun intended) you to go out and learn a whole lot more about this great American lawman. To that end I've listed three books in particular you should pick up. All are available at Amazon and worthy of your attention. In the meantime, saddle up for some rip-roaring adventure as you hit the outlaw trail with the greatest western lawman of all time, Deputy Marshal Bass Reeves.

Ron Fortier
Fort Collins, CO
10/19/2015

## -Bass Reeves Books-

***Black Gun, Silver: The Life and Legend of Frontier Marshal Bass Reeves (Race and Ethnicity in the American West)*** by Art T. Burton
The most complete, scholarly authenticated biography of the man.

***The Legend of Bass Reeves*** by Gary Paulsen
A somewhat romantic look at Reeve's exploits. Recommended for young adults.

***The Black Badge: Deputy United States Marshal Bass Reeves from Slave to Heroic Lawman*** by Paul L. Brady
Judge Paul L. Brady was appointed a Federal Administrative Law Judge and became the first African American to be so named. After serving 25 years on the bench, Judge Brady retired to write the story of his uncle, Bass Reeves.

# RIDE FROM THREE DEVILS

by Gary Phillips

Two men rode into Percussion. One had his head dipped and the other looked straight ahead. Their horses moved languidly along the main street, dry and dusty under the hooves of the animals. Soon they arrived at the Sheriff's office. The man in the lead swung his left leg over to his right, past his holstered Winchester rifle, and slid off his saddle onto the ground. He undid the reins of the trailing horse which had been bound to a metal loop sewn onto his saddle for just such a purpose. He re-tied these to a hitching post

"Let's go," the lead man said to the other one. Idly he scratched at the several days' growth of whiskers on his mustached face.

The second man lifted his head, also similarly whiskered. Squint-eyed he regarded the first man who waited; his face blank. He grumbled something unintelligible and he too dismounted. The shackles around his wrists rattled as he did so. They were heavy black iron restraints like what were used to march fresh inmates into territorial prisons.

"Bet this makes you feel like a big man, huh, boy?" The prisoner growled, shaking the shackles. "Got yourself a white man in chains makes you the head nigra, don't it?  Defying the natural order and all."

The lead man put a thumb and crooked forefinger to the brim of his hat and adjusted it as he looked up momentarily then back at the other one. It had been three days on the trail of this kind of talk and a man did have his limits he reckoned. He stepped forward and taking a hold of the links, pulled the prisoner forward.

"I said, let's go."

"Bass," Sheriff Lynde said as the two entered his office. He'd been watching them as he finished sweeping the floor.

"Rick," Reeves replied. He stepped to one side from the shackled man to not give him an opportunity to get the iron around his throat from behind. "This here is Barlow Oates wanted for horse rustling and selling stolen antiques." Reeves produced a folded wanted handbill and handed it across to the sheriff who had thinning blonde hair going to white.

"Four hundred dollars," the sheriff said reading the writ for Oates.

"And I earned every damn penny of it." Reeves unlocked and removed the metal from the other man's wrists.

Lynde, an older man hoping to make it to sixty, pointed toward his desk. "A telegram came for you this morning from Fort Smith." A torn scrap of tan paper lay on his desk, written out in neat handwriting in pencil by the town's telegraph operator.

"Am I to report in?" Reeves asked casually.

"I suppose. I'm not a busybody, Bass."

"Ain't sayin' you is, Rick. But you had to have read my name on it."

Two steps took him to the desk and he picked up the transmission. As he frowned at it, Oates spoke.

"When I get out, nigger, I'm going to look you up. I want you to sleep with one eye open not knowing when that's going to be, but I'll be right over you 'fore I slit yer throat."

The shackles made a sound in Reeves' hand. "I'll see you, Rick."

"Always a pleasure, Bass."

To Reeves' back Oates continued. "Then when I'm done with you, I'm going to start in rough on that wife of yours you mentioned. Let her know what a real man feels like."

The sheriff clucked his tongue and stepped back as Reeves stopped, twirled around, and lashed the shackles across Oates' face. He dropped to the wooden flooring like he'd been shot, his broken nose bleeding onto his mouth. His hat had flown off his head and landed at the foot of the potbelly stove in the corner.

The sheriff helped the groaning man to his feet as Bass Reeves left the office to get a soak and a shave.

The winter sun was high overhead providing little warmth as territorial deputy marshal Bass Reeves guided his mount forward. He cut through a sea of green and yellow sawgrass languidly swaying before him as yet another frigid breeze tickled the lamb wool collar of his coat. His horse shook its head and he patted the beast's neck.

"Yeah, I know, snow's coming" he muttered.

Reeves assessed the landscape, deeply breathing in the crisp air. Before him was his destination, the Cypress Swamp, so named for its preponderance of that type of tree bordering and woven throughout the boggy area. Even if he were blind, he noted as he got closer, he'd know he was near as the temperature rose and mosquitoes buzzed about even though this was not the season for them. Tucked in his shirt pocket was a folded up paper, a wanted bulletin for one William Crawford also known as Alamosa Bill. Among the ex-Army sharpshooter's stated offenses as had been explained to Reeves by Marshal Fagan was safe blowing and seduction. Reeves grinned wanly beneath his brush mustache. Seduction, now did that mean he'd been sparkin' some captain's lonely wife?

"That Indian palaverin' you do will came in handy on this, Bass," Fagan, a large man given to bluster but who could back it up, had said to him at his office in Fort Smith near the federal prison. Reeves had ridden in to take the assignment after receiving the summons by telegram. "He was last seen in Briscoe getting a few provisions."

Reeves had nodded. Briscoe was a settlement in the Choctaw lands where whites and Indians did some trading and intermingling. "I know somebody around there that might be helpful," he'd said.

In particular Reeves was desirous of capturing his quarry as there was currently a reward of $4,700 on his head. A fantastic sum as far as Reeves was concerned. There had been larger bounties, but not too many. The reason for the sizeable amount, put up mostly by railroad barons, was a Pinkerton had been killed as a result of the latest commission of one of Crawford's crimes. This was the robbery of a federal payroll shipment being transported by stagecoach for distribution to several Army posts. Crawford, and an associate named Johan Tinderoot of Swedish extraction, had pulled off the heist. The two actually managed not to kill anyone though did badly pistol whip one of the shipment's guards.

The Pinkerton man had followed up on a lead and tracked down Tinderoot, who apparently had some sort of religious conversion after a life of bad behavior. Tinderoot had used his portion of the money realized on the robbery to settle in Guthrie, and help build a Lutheran church there. He gave up without resistance when confronted, and willingly told all he knew about the habits and proclivities of his former saddle pal, Alamosa Bill – an individual he hadn't been in touch with since the payroll robbery more than a year before.

Nonetheless, the dogged Pink kept after Crawford; seemingly compelled in a rather personal way, some observed. For his effort, the detective was shot in the head one Tuesday morning as he crossed the street in the town of Muddy River on his way from the livery stable to breakfast in the only hotel there. The recovered bullet, from what remained of the Pinkerton's brainpan, was extracted by a doctor who readily recognized the .50-70 round. It originated from a Sharps carbine rifle, standard issue during the Civil War on both sides of the conflict. The doctor had been a combat surgeon then and while often taking a nip or two of cherry brandy before 11 a.m. most days due to the continuing nightmares of that time, his haunted memories made such identification uncontested.

It was later determined the killing shot had come from some 250 yards away originating atop the Stanhope bordello at the other end of the main street. These facts were prominent in Reeves' mind as he entered the swamp. There was no specific reason that Crawford should know he was on his trail, but he must know of the amount out on him the marshal reasoned and be on the lookout. Idly, Reeves swatted at a bug feasting on his face as he eased his horse into a thicket of overgrowth. He halted and dismounted.

On foot, the reins in his hand, Reeves went further in, weaving his way through the thick stands of the cypress trees, their scented leaves not only overhead but on a good number of the trunks descending almost down to the base. He had a rough idea where he was heading, though this was his first time in this place. That was due to information gained from a friend of his, George R. Snake Catcher, a Choctaw whom Reeves had employed in the past for his tracking skills.

"I'll draw you a map," Snake Cather had said in his native tongue. "It's been awhile since I've been in there, but for an old man I remember pretty good. I'll go over it with you," he added diplomatically knowing the other man was illiterate.

"I appreciate that, George," Reeves had replied, also in the Choctaw language. The two smoked cheroots on the porch of the former's modest adobe and wood home on his small pig farm outside Briscoe. "The way it is in there, no surprise there's no real village or anything like that, but my reckoning is the folk that populate the swamp are very clannish."

"A good number of inbreeds I'm bettin'," his friend observed laconically.

"Overseen by a witchy woman calls herself Mama Crow," Snake Cather added.

His sister-in-law, and sometimes second wife, poked her head out of the house. "You're staying the night, aren't you, Bass?" Betty Snake Cather asked him. In her forties, she was a few years older than Reeves' 38 but a handsome woman with still coal black hair and alert dark eyes. Her gaze lingered on the relaxed lawman.

"Yes, the barn is fine."

"You sure?" she said.

George Snake Catcher watched his puffs of smoke rise toward the crooked beams of the overhang.

"My wife for sure thinks so, Betty."

She shifted the colorful shawl around her shoulders. She and her sister were daughters of a mingo, a local chief, and used to getting their way.

"You're no stranger to Indian customs, Bass. Let me know if you get cold."

"Yes ma'am." Bass nodded, his cigar dangling from the corner of his mouth.

Focusing on the present, Reeves got to a ribbon of water and took out the second piece of folded up paper he carried, Snake Catcher's map. Unfolding it the horse nuzzled him and he patted his head. Though Reeves couldn't cipher words as he would admit, he did understand markings such as arrows for direction, dash lines and most importantly to his chosen profession, or at least his other undertaking than being a horse rancher, he knew that four places of numbers like with Crawford meant a big payday. He also by necessity commanded a sizeable memory so if a word was important, he'd have someone read it to him and he'd call up its meaning while recognizing the sequence of its letter forms. He did this now with the few words on Snake Catcher's map. This was easier as the words were not in a string as in a sentence, but not more than three words together in different parts of the map drawn on foolscap.

Satisfied from his consultation of the crude map, he put it away and walked north, following the tributary. Sure enough, this brought him to a larger body of water bordered by the grove of cypress and a few other types of trees and thick foliage. Looking about, getting his bearings, he tethered his horse to a squat shrub and went to his saddlebag. He removed a few carrots and a hardtack biscuit bound in a piece of cloth he'd shredded from a worn bed sheet. The carrots in the palm of his hand he fed to the horse who gobbled them up greedily. He unwrapped the hardtack, which had been rolled in salt, and gave that to his horse as well.

It had been Reeves' experience that if you took care of your mount, then the horse had good feelings about you when it counted – like being chased and fired at by an owlhoot or two and getting away at top speed was a priority. He certainly knew better than to let his animal drink swamp water, what with all manner of tiny critters in it carrying all manner of sicknesses. His wife Nellie had read something in the newspaper about these creepy-crawlies called germs, so damn small you couldn't see them with the naked eye but were the way maladies like anthrax or influenza spread invisible-like in the air. Give him a quarry he could eyeball and lay hands on any time.

He had a swallow from his canteen. Finding clean water for his horse was one more matter on his mind as he left his coat with the animal—as the swamp had its own temperature, a tolerable humidity hovering about these environs. Reeves went into a thicket of greenery and made his way to the river's edge. He needed to get where it was better traveling by water than on foot. His arms and face were already itching from various annoying fresh red welts attracting more of these damnable mosquitoes. Time was a factor, *but wasn't it always?* he reasoned, as he pressed on.

Yet, as Snake Catcher had advised, there at the bend in the bank was a shack that looked as if a strong wind to come along, it would surely fall down. There was a rough-hewn dock. Tethered next to it were two canoes, made with hide, bobbing in the water.

"Are you a Negro?" came a voice from the shack.

"I'm a marshal," said Reeves as he stopped before the rickety porch of the abode. He had only one of his single action Colts strapped on. He hooked his thumbs in his cartridge belt to look relaxed but could reach the weapon in a blink.

Out stepped a white individual in clothes so threadbare, it could only be the dirt and grease coating them that held the pants and shirt together, Reeves surmised. The bandy-legged man in them might by fifty or he could be eighty. A patch of spiky white hair decorated the top of his head. He wore round spectacles and chawed on a tear of tobacco. The man cradled a shotgun but didn't have it pointed at his visitor.

"That a fact?" he said.

"I hear you rent out your canoes from time to time."

"Who says?'

"George Snake Catcher."

The old boy spit out a stream of black juice. "Do tell?"

"We cut trail together some in the past."

The other man studied Reeves then blurted out, "Two dollar."

"Heard it was more like four bits."

"Two dollar," he repeated mildly.

Reeves considered asking was that the black price but handed the bills over. With that the canoe man walked back into his shack and shut the door.

The deputy marshal went to the dock, gingerly stepping across its creaking planks that more than once threatened to give way to his footfalls. He was glad one of the canoes had a paddle in it as he didn't relish searching around or asking for one from the disagreeable proprietor. He got the canoe undone and settling himself, started paddling away. He was going toward where Snake Catcher's map indicated was the compound of Mama Crow. From her Reeves hoped to glean a clue as to where Alamosa Bill might have gotten to after being on his trail for two weeks now. That he'd headed in here had been an educated guess on his and George Snake Catcher's part. There wasn't much in this part of the territory except Briscoe and the Cypress Swamp. These weren't generally locals on the way to somewhere elsewhere so it followed that Alamosa Bill had come in here for a reason. Maybe to hide out, but Reeves and his friend had doubted that as his goal.

He got turned around once. The shoreline looked the same in many sections and if the terrain wasn't broken up with trees gnarled in specific ways or distinct boulders, the whole of it had a visual monotony. But doubling back he paid better attention to the water and spied the ridged back of a gator disappear among a low hang of cypress boughs and leaves. Following the creature, he was on the tributary he'd been told about and soon came to a clearing. Before him was a larger, more formal looking residence than the canoe man's shack. A dock in better shape than the previous one jutted into the river as well, and several smaller shacks and lean-tos radiated from the main structure. Planking and four-by-fours had been placed on the muddy earth to provide better footing. Reeves inhaled a certain aroma and watched a thin column of white smoke drift upward from behind one of the lean-tos. It seemed Mama Crow and her kinfolk dealt in corn liquor among other pursuits.

He heard rustling in the foliage and was that a giggle? But no one stepped into the open. The good-sized man stood up in the canoe to his six-foot-plus height and called out.

"My name is Bass Reeves and I'm looking for an hombre who goes by Alamosa Bill." Pointedly he hadn't beached the conveyance and if need be, was prepared to dive off of it into the brackish water. He'd take his chance with a hungry gator versus flying lead.

"Whatchu want him fer, colored man?" a male voice called back. He also heard a "Shush," by a different voice…female if he was pressed to identify the maker.

The voices had come from his right and Reeves slightly turned that way in the gently bobbing canoe. "Kind of a personal matter," he said, stretching the truth some. He'd decided it was best if these people in here didn't know he was a lawman as no matter what his hue, they probably didn't cotton much to that sort of undertaking. And it was kind of personal in a way. His lion's share of the reward money would go far on his farm in terms of needed repairs, feeding his livestock and his and Nellie's offspring who insisted on continuing to outgrow their clothes and shoes. Hand-me-downs only went so far.

"I can pay for the information."

A silence dragged then appeared a lanky so-and-so at least five inches taller than Reeves. He was dressed atypically in black pants and coat with badly frayed cuffs, no shirt, with a dented top hat cocked at a rakish angle on his head. Colorful feathers splayed from the hat's band. He had an elongated face and deep-set eyes beneath a heavy brow. He carried a six-shooter at the ready. Next to him was an old woman with a hawk nose in a gingham dress who held onto a cane with a fancy silver head though Reeves couldn't determine what it depicted. She also had on round glasses with blue lenses.

"My Kenroy asked why you want this man," the woman he figured was Mama Crow said. Since the bean pole Kenroy had let it slip that Crawford had been through, she didn't see no reason to use pretense, Reeves concluded.

"I'd rather not say as it involves my sister and well, it's a family concern." Maybe saying this would generate some tender feelings from them he angled.

"You aim on shooting him?" She pointed her cane at his sidearm.

"Not if I can help it," he said truthfully. He held up two three-dollar gold pieces. "Like I said, I can pay."

The tall man looked down at the old woman who, despite her cane, stood straight. She motioned Reeves to come to shore. He did and standing before her, saw how commanding her grey eyes were; like a sky pregnant with thunder and ruination. She held up an open palm and he placed the coins on it. She curled her fingers around the money making a tight, steady fist.

"He was here but he's gone now." Like the canoe man, she wheeled about, ready to go.

"What did he want and which direction did he go?'

The old lady didn't turn back but the one called Kenroy did. "You sure ask a lot, mister."

"I paid more than fair for some tradin'."

"He was desirous of my specialty," the old woman said.

"And that would be?"

She glanced back at him. "The ways beyond men and this world."

For the first time Reeves noted that carved into the surfaces of the main house and the other structures were specific shapes and symbols reminding him of those he'd seen Indian medicine men scribe in the dirt prior to a ceremony. "You do a spell or a charm for him, is that it, Mama Crow?"

Now she turned back, smiling with teeth missing. "You ain't as slow as you look."

"That way he went," the tall one said, pointing north. "The way you can go too."

North meant following the river but he didn't want to leave his horse, he was going to need him once he was out of here. It was late afternoon and Reeves decided what he was going to do as he got back in the canoe. He'd paddle some more up river and see what he might see. Crawford knew about the price on his head but he wouldn't particularly think anyone was on his trail. Maybe he'd stopped to rest or who knew what, but Reeves concluded the best course was to explore more as he was yet to have any sense where Alamosa Bill might be headed.

Back on the prime stretch of river, Reeves couldn't shake the feeling he was being observed. A time or two he'd seen movement through the trees but maybe it was a reflection of sunlight or this place was getting under his skin. He passed under a blossoming bough and two snakes dropped down on him.

"Shit," he swore as he bolted upright, tipping the small boat over and sending him and the creatures into the water. His hasty glance informed him the reptiles were water moccasins, also called cottonmouths. Unfortunate for humans and animals, the damn things were deadly in the water or on the land. He managed to evade a strike and grabbed the attacking snake by its body just below the back of the head. The large jaw of the four foot killer hinged open as it hissed and poison secreted from its fangs. Kicking his legs to stay afloat, Reeves searched about for the other one but didn't see any ripples in the water.

The cottonmouth coiled about his forearm. He swung the snake in hand around by the tail and thumped the head down on the side of the overturned canoe. He did this several times, hoping to thoroughly stun the cottonmouth. Far from the shore, he had to get out of the water.

*Reeves couldn't shake the feeling he was being observed.*

Reeves threw the dazed snake away from him and swam to fetch the canoe floating away from him. He got to it and righted it, all the time wary for the bite from that missing second snake. The canoe had water in it and rode low on the river. If he got in it the thing would sink but he had to have it. He made for the shore, pushing it along as he swam furiously.

Peripherally he sensed movement and damn him but an alligator was gliding toward him from the other side of the canoe. Reeves had no chance to make it to land ahead of the beast so he stopped and treading water, bent below the surface. He got the hunting knife tucked inside his boot in his grip just as the gator closed in again. But he was still between the canoe and him and had paused as well, calculating how best to make a meal of his warm-blooded entree. The gator submerged and Reeves repeatedly stabbed at the water, striking the big reptile's tough hide. This caused the amphibian to veer off at least temporarily and he swam with everything he had to get to the shore.

The gator reversed course back at Reeves as he dragged himself onto the mud and muck. He threw his knife aside and crawling, got on his knees and grabbed a stout branch lying nearby. The gator now was on the land and scrambled toward Reeves, its big mouth open and ready. His own mouth set in a grim line, Reeves was on his feet, side-stepped the attacking beast, and drove the sharp end of the branch into the creature's eye. The big reptile roared and snapped its powerful rows of razor-like teeth. Reeves got his weight behind the branch and drove the shaft into the predator's single-minded brain.

The gleam of life went out behind the gator's other eye and it lay still on its belly. Reeves swallowed big gulps of air through his open mouth, his chest rising and falling rapidly. Soon his breathing was under control and straightening up, he heard someone or something nearby and unlimbered his gun, which had remained holstered. The gunpowder in the cartridges was probably too wet to fire but he took comfort in having it in his hand anyway. He looked around and saw where he'd plunged his knife into the earth and shook it loose, re-holstering his sidearm. He didn't for a minute believe those two snakes just happened to be up in the same tree and fall on him. He edged forward, wary and ready.

He heard that high-pitched annoying giggle again. "That you, Mama Crow? Come to see about your handiwork?"

He turned his head this way and that, eyes probing the cloying emerald density of the mangrove. It was getting on dark. Reeves needed to build a fire to dry himself and his gun out. Sweeping aside a thatch of low hanging palmetto, he came before a flat area. He went back toward the shoreline and dragged the canoe back to this area. It was getting cool and he started to shiver. Using his knife, he managed to hack away enough branches and stripped them of their leaves and then cut and tore them in halves and quarters.

Racing the fading light, he then constructed a small teepee of the wood over a nest of bark shavings. Rubbing a thin branch between his palms, its end on a piece of flat wood beneath it, he got enough friction and heat going to ignite the tuft of inner bark under the flat piece. As the tuft, like the consistency of fine fur, smoked he picked it up and blew on this. It caught fully on fire and this he placed on the shavings inside his teepee. Soon he had a decent fire going and was able to add to it with larger pieces of wood. He stripped down naked, warmer than being in his freezing clothes. He laid his wet items as close as he could to the fire, watching to make sure a spark didn't set them ablaze as well.

Lighting a few longer branches he lashed together with baby branches, he used this as a torch to see the way back to the gator's body, dragging the canoe. He secured the other end of the lit branches in the muddy ground and knocking away flies, rolled the gator over on its back and cut into its belly. He put the slices of gator meat in the canoe, and torch back in hand, dragged this back to his makeshift camp. He chopped the meat up into manageable sizes and spearing the goods, roasted them over the fire. Gator had a certain gaminess to it and was by no means his favorite, but it would do he mused as he munched on his dinner.

"Ay-hee," a voice called out.

Reeves, on a knee was up and spun about with his knife in hand. Just beyond the glow of the fire danced a compact form. This individual skittered about, arms and legs flailing, jumping and whirling as if trying to match the randomness of the crackling flames.

"Don't be shy," he said. "Hell, I'm the one in his birthday suit."

The figure stopped. In marked contrast to his previous state, he, and the marshal was pretty sure it was male, now stood stone still, hands at his sides like a soldier at attention.

Reeves held up some of his gator "Oh, excuse my manners." He snuggled into his semi-dry longjohns and again held up the reptile delight. The figure inched forward and he could see it was a boy of maybe ten or older. He was barefoot and dressed in material that was more tatters than clothes. That he was a product of inbreeding was evident to Reeves with his elongated head similar but more pronounced than Kenroy's. His thin brown hair was already nearly gone and one side of his face was asymmetrical to the opposite side.

"Good, see." Reeves munched on a corner of his catch and took it off his homemade spit. He held it out for the boy. "Come on, have some."

The child loped forward in a sideways gait, swinging his arms like an orangutan the bounty man had seen once in a traveling circus. He gobbled up the morsel, a smile breaking out on his placid face.

"I'm Bass," he said, jabbing his thumb on his chest. "Bass," he repeated. Calling himself Mr. Reeves didn't seem like the way to go with this kid he reasoned. "Who are you?"

The swamp boy held out his hand and Reeves gave him more food. "Ocee" he said as he chewed open-mouthed.

Okay, he could talk and understand. Reeves asked, "Ocee, you see any other strangers today?"

Again the hand came out and again Reeves obliged. His head bobbed up and down.

"Alamosa?"

That got nothing. Reeves worried his bottom lip. Then he pointed at his hat on the ground which he'd saved it from floating away then the canoe had tipped over. "Hat, Ocee, he have a hat like that?"

Now he did nod in the affirmative. Aside from Kenroy, he'd noticed the folk in here didn't wear hats to protect against the sun given the light was filtered pleasantly through the leaf-laden boughs. Chuckling he added, "He didn't happen to say where he was headed, huh, Ocee?"

The kid was busy licking gator grease off his fingers.

Reeves put the remaining portions of the gator strips on his spit and started roasting that up, adding wood to the fire. "Ah, what the hell, we'll eat good tonight, Ocee."

"What the hell," the kid imitated. He said it in a deep voice, maybe mimicking Reeves. Or maybe…

Intently Reeves stared at the boy, conscious he didn't want to scare him. "The man in the hat, he say that?"

Ocee stepped closer, his dull eyes coming alive in the flickering light. He puffed out his chest and said in his pretend adult voice, "What the hell, Mama Crow, needs me a good charm for Three Devils."

Reeves grinned broadly and broke out in laughter. "You done acquit yourself right good, Ocee, yes sir, right good."

The kid laughed too, a high-pitched screech that could curdle milk.

In the morning as Reeves padded away, Ocee stood on the bank watching him go, petting the second cottonmouth along its slick body which was curled around his arm, pet-like.

The horse's tracks through the slush of light snow weren't deep. The flurry had been more wet than solid matter as Bass Reeves arrived on the outskirts of Three Devils four days after departing Cypress Swamp. The sun had been up about half an hour. He'd shaved his head, trimmed his brush mustache considerably, donned black pants and vest, white starched collarless shirt. He also had on a pair of steel-rimmed, owlish glasses with blue lenses and a weathered top hat with colorful feather sticking out of its band. He was passing through a work camp mostly of tents large and small of workers and what have you on the ever-expanding M, K, & T rail line. He saw whites and blacks going about and even a smattering of Chinese and Indians.

Through the billowing flap of one tent, he got a glimpse inside of a man having sex with a woman. She was bent forward, holding onto a hard-backed chair that creaked with their combined efforts. He had his pants down around his ankles and between grunts swigged on some whisky. Her ruffled dress was bunched up but no private parts were visible. The woman, a hard-eyed handsome freckled brunette, looked over at Reeves and smiled sweetly. He tipped his hat to the lady and kept on. He stopped at the smell of fresh coffee brewing and eggs frying in pork grease. His horse whinnied, appreciating the smell too. This was one of the few wooden buildings though many of the larger tents had planking down over the muddy ground. More than one horse was hitched outside the no name café and Reeves planned to join the assembled inside. Set at a right angle to the restaurant was another structure where Reeves heard the familiar clackty-clack of a telegraph key in operation. He looked up to see a telegraph pole next to the building with twin wires running away from it in two directions. He then entered to the din of gruff laughter and utensils clanking against plates. Seating was bench style and it took him a moment to figure out where to order.

"Just ground up some quail this morning," the big-armed man behind the front counter told the disguised marshal when he came forward.

"Okay, gimme a quail patty, bacon, three eggs, scrambled, and, flapjacks, two, no three I'd say and some coffee."

The counter man looked off for a moment, his lips moving as he added up the cost. "Sixty cents," he said while he wrote the order down on a small pad of paper with a pencil that had teeth marks on it.

Reeves counted out the coins and handed them across. He then strolled about, hoping to hear a conversation that might prove valuable to him before he got into Three Devils proper. It didn't take long.

"...don't know what I was thinking," a man with a heavy Irish accent was saying to two others as he slurped his coffee.

"That lime-juicer sure knows how to keep his pockets lined," one of the man's breakfast companions agreed. "If he don't get you at one of his faro tables, then them saloon gals of his take it out in trade."

The third one observed, "Yeah, but last week I was with one of them and those tits of hers would make a parson want to sin." He shook his head appreciatively at the memory.

Reeves moved on and got to a bench where several black men ate. "Mind if I have a squat?" he asked.

"Naw, come on cousin," one of the men said, scooting over some. He was a burly individual who ate with his left hand and kept his right forearm curved some around his plate, as if guarding his food.

"You're new around here," one of the other men said. One of the eyes in his head was filmed over.

"Just passing through, on my way into town."

The dead-eyed man exchanged a look with the burly one who made a sound in his throat. "You gunhawks just can smell it, huh?" He said referring to the Colt Peacemaker nestled in a well-worn holster on the stranger's hip.

One of the waitresses, a Cherokee woman with a limp, brought Reeves' food. He tipped her two bits. "Thank you," he said in the Cherokee language, handing her the quarter.

She gave a nod and returned to the kitchen

"You got me at a disadvantage,' Reeves replied, slathering butter on his pancakes.

"I don't mean nothin', mister" the burly one answered easily. "I'm not one for stickin' my nose where it don't belong."

"I don't mean nothin' either. Fella just likes to know the lay of the land is all. Where the potholes might be less his horse steps in one and comes up hobbled."

There was a fourth man at the table who hadn't talked. His breakfast wasn't done but he got up and moved to another table. The dead-eyed man watched him go, chewing on a biscuit.

The burly man continued, "Mister, we just here to lay tracks and get in a poke now and then when we can. What that big wheel in town Macnee has in mind is y'all's business." He attacked his stack of four pancakes and a pork chop again.

"I hear you." Reeves knew better than to press his curiosity but from what was implicated; this Macnee was gathering some gunmen for who knew what specifically, but clearly some big job he planned. This had to be why Crawford had come this way and he might have a friend or two in town who might not cotton to Reeves coming along looking to capture the wanted hombre. He needed to know more about this honcho but it wouldn't be from these two. They passed the rest of the time mostly in silence as they ate and belched.

Afterward Reeves took a walk through camp. He saw what he presumed to be the telegraph man leave what he now realized was both the telegraph office and a kind of temporary train depot as on the opposite side there was a raw plywood platform fronting the tracks. He guessed he was the telegraph man as he had on sleeve protectors on both arms, worn to prevent pencil smudges from dirtying your clothes. Reeves also made sure to water and feed his horse. While there was no formal sporting house as far as he could tell, he circled back to the freckle-faced woman wringing out linens behind the tent where she'd been holding onto the chair.

"Hey, sugah," she cooed. "Let me finish this and we can sit a spell and have us some tea."

*So that's what they're calling it these days*, Reeves reflected. He showed the last three-dollar gold piece he had. "Over that there tea, I'll make it worth your while to tell me all you know about this fella called Macnee."

"What makes you think I know what's what?" She sounded nonchalant but her gaze was locked on the gold piece.

"That dresser of yours." He'd managed to also notice that when he rode past earlier.

"How you mean?"

"Pretty fancy piece for this camp I was pondering," Reeves noted. "Now you being a lady I'm sure you like nice things but in a place like this, seems to me you'd be worried some drunk gandy dancer might fall into it one night and bust it all up." It was a hunch, but he'd guessed she might be new to the camp. That if she was setting up shop, why out here and not in town where there'd be more customers and less exposure to the elements? Unless she had no choice.

She placed a clothespin on the line holding a sheet fast, regarding him. "Who are you?

He held up the gold piece again. "A man willing to pay you good for a smidgen of your time and you ain't gotta earn it on your back…or bent over." He smiled and so did the woman. In her tent with pallets for flooring, they sat and indeed sipped tea so dark green it was almost black. And Brandyrose as she called herself, told him what she knew about the transplanted Englishman Carnaby Macnee and his enterprises in Three Devils.

"A beer sounds about right," Reeves said to the barman. He stood at the bar in Faro Jack's, a large structure that dominated a side street off the main one in Three Devils. It was a combination casino, saloon and two-story hotel. While this was early afternoon, there were several patrons about and a few dance hall gals floating around in frilly dresses.

Reeves put a quarter down when his beer arrived and he sipped it slowly, taking in his surroundings. He hadn't seen Alamosa Bill but did recognize an individual he was fairly certain had until recently, been doing a stint in the Yuma territorial prison. He was sitting at a corner table with two others playing rounds of Blackjack. This confirmed what he'd learned from Brandyrose, that within the last two weeks, several owlhoots had come to town and were bedded down at Faro Jack's.

"I said have a seat, girly," a voice commanded.

Reeves and the others in the bar looked at a skinny man with a wide hat grab the arm of one of the women. She pulled her arm back.

"You've had enough, mister," she said.

The obviously drunk man glared back at her with pin-pointed eyes. "You too good to sit on my lap, that it? Shit, your job is to please the customers."

The barman came from around the bar and toward the abrasive cowpuncher. "Take your hands off her."

It happened quicker than one would have imagined an inebriate could act. From his seat he clubbed the barman in the head with the butt of his gun and now, weaving some, was on his feet and had hold of the woman. He waved his gun about.

"I hear 'nother word from any damn body and I'll plug ya. Me and this here…damsel, got us some affectioning ta do." He turned his head and leered at her.

Reeves' beer mug hit him square in his temple and he sagged to the floor. Moving as he threw his glass, he got to the downed man and stepped on the wrist of his gun hand as it twitched. "No you don't." Reeves bent and liberated the six-shooter from the drunk who swore at him.

"Thas' what we get for freeing you ungrateful black-hided sonsabitches. My dear old brother lost his leg in the War and look at the thanks I get." He started sobbing.

"Bravo, bravo," came a new voice coupled with a deliberate, slow hand clap from above.

Reeves looked up to see a man with blonde hair going gray at the temples standing in a silk robe and ascot at the mezzanine level-railing overlooking the bar area. "Quite the knight-errand you are, sir."

"I'll take the credit," Reeves said, "but self-preservation probably spurred my hand more."

The other man held his arms wide. "Who can argue with self-preservation?" Then, to the barman who had recovered: "Once you see to the riff-raff occupying my floor, Sid, see that this fellow, ah, I say, what's your name, old son?"

"Ben, Mister Macnee, Ben Jeffers."

"Ah, you've heard of me?'

"Yes, sir, I have." Reeves didn't want to lay it on too thick, making an outright pitch to join his gang. He knew from past experience he had to make it look as natural as he could otherwise the boss man would want to know why Reeves wanted in – what had he heard? Who sent him? Those sorts of questions would be asked and unless he had satisfying answers, a bullet in his brain pan could result.

"Outstanding." He produced a cigar from his robe's pocket and sparked a wooden match to life by swiping it against the base of a hanging kerosene lamp he steadied. "As I was saying Sid, see to it that Jeffers here has what he wants to drink and eat, for today." He chuckled as he turned and went back along the upper corridor.

"Thank you, darlin'" the saloon girl said, briefly touching his arm. She was young and pale white and tawny-haired.

"Pleasure, ma'am," he replied, touching the brim of his dented top hat. That Three Devils was a wide open town was evident by a white women—granted a girl getting commissions on how many drinks the visitors to Faro Jack's bought her—touching him without such causing a ruckus, and the noted absence of a sheriff or deputies. She sashayed away like a more experienced woman than her twenty years would suggest, Reeves estimated.

*"I say, what's your name, old son?"*

He made sure to nurse his beers and was pleasantly surprised that the roast beef sandwich he ate was better than the usual bar grub. The meat wasn't near spoiled as was often the case and the bread was spongy, moist, not dry and tasteless. Later, he was munching on a pickled egg, a drummer who sold pots, pans and scissors was chatting him up about the benefits of buffalo steaks, apparently an item he was also peddling, when a hand came down on his shoulder.

"Damn, thought that was you," said the newcomer, a bemused look on his face.

He quickly eliminated any surprise he was showing as he turned around to see a beaming Nat Love. He was a handsome, copper-colored, half black, half Cherokee rangy man with an easy smile and knuckles the size of flatted quarters. "Well, how-dee, damn if it ain't you, Nat. How the hell you been, man?" He shook his hand while with the other had it on the back of his shoulders.

"Fine, just fine."

Before his friend could answer and possibly make a mistake and say his actual name, Reeves interjected. "Say, uh, sorry, I didn't catch your name, mister" he said to the traveling salesman.

"Howard Peevity."

"Well, I'm Ben Jeffers, Mister Peevity, and this here is the famous ramrodder, rodeo sharp shooter and all around outdoorsman Nat Love." He said this louder than necessary; hoping to emphasize his pretend name should anyone being paying attention to them.

"Pleased," Love drawled, giving Reeves a sideway glance. "Been awhile… Ben."

"Yes it has. What brings you to town?"

Love cocked his hat back some from his head of long black curly hair. It fell to the nape of his neck. "Just delivered a passel of prize Brahmans for shipping out to K.C.," he said. "Figured to whet my whistle so to speak." His head had turned as he gazed at the young woman who the belligerent patron had bothered earlier. She carried a drink in each hand to a table of solemn men playing poker. The casino had formally opened and the regular doorman was on duty. He sat in a chair that gave him a view of the entrance, a shotgun resting across his lap.

In a while the drummer checked his pocket watch and excused himself from the two. The men moved to a table tucked partially under the stairs as the late afternoon crowd began to file in. The roulette wheel spun, that particular sound of the marble bouncing around it could be heard above the growing din.

"What you up to, Bass?" Nat Love asked him while he rolled a cigarette. "Want one?' he offered.

"No thanks." He was both anxious and relieved to have encountered Love. The man was more than able with a shootin' iron he knew and the way things were sizing up he might have need of his services. In addition to the former Yuma resident, he'd seen two other gunmen, one of whom he'd met before, briefly. Though he didn't figure this man would recall him given how he'd altered his appearance. But Love wasn't a sentimentalist. He didn't work for free. And rightly, Reeves wouldn't ask a man to risk his life without recompense.

"I'm not rightly sure at the moment,' he said truthfully.

Love held up his hands. "Ain't meant to get in your business. But when I first seen you in that there get-up, I realized you was here on the quiet-like for a reason."

"I am."

Love got his cigarette lit and blew a thin stream of smoke into the room.

"Look, you know I'm not a greedy man, Nat, well, hell, less than some you and I've run up on anyway."

"I hear what you're sayin', Bass. Man starts a job, man wants to finish that job." He had the cigarette dangling from a corner of his mouth, its smoke trailing up past his amber eyes. "Especially a man who's got hisself youngins' to feed and care for."

"You shoving out tomorrow?"

"Maybe, maybe not. Depends, you know how that be." He grinned broadly at him. "Course, could be you don't remember given you been tied to them apron strings so long."

Love rose and stretched. "I'm'a go blow some of my hard-earned cash on faro. I was in San Francisco last winter and this here gal I met there showed me a trick or two that might come in handy."

"We still talking about cards?" Reeves jibed.

Love winked at him and walked over to the faro table. Reeves returned to the bar, intending to get a stiff belt and puzzle more on what Macnee was planning and would that interfere with his getting a hold of Crawford – who had entered the establishment while he and Love had talked. He too was at the bar drinking. Off to one side, Reeves saw the former Yuma prisoner flirting with a good-sized, pretty saloon gal he heard called Big Edna.

Carnaby Macnee finally made his appearance. Reeves was sipping his whiskey when the Englishman came down the stairs. About an hour before a woman around thirty with dark blue eye shadow now running the roulette wheel had gone up with a tray of food for him. He knew from Brandyrose her name was Collette O'Brien. She was the reason for the prostitute's exit from town. Brandyrose hadn't been all that forthcoming about details but from what Reeves had pieced together, Macnee had been getting a might too friendly with the street walker and O'Brien had put her foot down about such.

"Jealous bitch," Brandyrose had groused.

Reeves had diplomatically kept a straight face when she uttered this but had nodded his head understandingly.

Macnee was dressed in a grey suit, red vest, with a black cravat over a green shirt. He hair was combed just so and Reeves had the impression when the man sweated, it probably smelled like rose water. The impresario went over to Crawford and the two made small talk. Soon Reeves watched as Macnee signaled one of the working girls, an amply endowed young woman, and she and the grinning sharpshooter ascended the stairs together.

The Britisher then made the rounds, glad handing and laughing, chit-chatting briefly, slapping backs and whispering in this or that ear. There was one individual he spoke to for several minutes. This was a sallow complexioned, pinched faced man with limp hair. He sat alone with a beer at a small table along with several sheets of foolscap before him he'd been scribbling on, Reeves had noted. The two talked until Macnee got up from the table and went to say hello to the doorman and on to some men playing faro including the telegraph operator Reeves had seen earlier at the work camp. Now he was hanging around the roulette table pretending to be interested in the game. But this also allowed him to overhear some of Macnee's conversation. He was talking to the telegraph man.

"You make sure when Mr. Goodhew arrives tomorrow, you get him over here pronto, Tom. No delays."

"Sure thing, Mr. Macnee. Your man delivered the buckboard earlier."

"That's right, we're going to show him we're top notch around here."

Seems Tom the telegraph man doubled as the part-time station man as well. Reeves had an inkling as to who this Goodhew fellow was Macnee anticipated. It might be nothing, but then again, he might have a way into the gang and be better able to realize his bounty.

Less than half an hour later Reeves prepared to leave. He had a few matters to attend to before tomorrow.

"Watch it," the pinch faced man groused at a cowboy who, backing up, had bumped the table, sending some of his papers to the ground.

"Sorry, there...bookkeeper," he said off-handedly. The cowhand had his arm around one of the saloon girl's waist, and they chuckled, both of them tipsy. As they tried to get steady on their feet, he put his hand on the table for leverage. Pushing up, the young woman leaning against him, their combined weight upended the table. The papers were strewn about haphazardly.

"Goddamit, you stupid hayseed," the man with the limp hair yelled.

The other man, taller with wide shoulders, stared drunkenly at the other one who was no more than five-six. He and the woman looked at each other wide-eyed and started laughing uproariously.

The smaller man now had a large knife in his hand as if granted a silent wish by an avenging angel. He came at the startled, unarmed cow puncher but a gunshot froze all concerned in the sporting house.

"That'll be enough, Georgie," Macnee said pleasantly. He wasn't the one who shot the round into the air. Next to him was the woman in blue eye shadow, Collette O'Brien. She had a derringer in her hand and seemed quite comfortable in its use.

"Sorry, Mr. Macnee,' the saloon girl in his employ said.

"Think nothing of it, darling." He said soothingly, a hand on the one he'd called Georgie's shoulder. "My friend here thinks too deeply is all." The hand squeezed hard. "Isn't that right, Georgie?"

"Yes, I...I didn't mean anything."

The table was righted and the knife placed upon it. Reeves could see it was a Bowie sort with a square handle, like the kind Confederate soldiers were issued during the War, he recalled. He'd sharpened and shined a fair amount of them when enslaved under the Colonel before he escaped to freedom during that time.

The tension evaporated and Reeves, snuggling into his sheep hide coat lined in lamb's wool, went out into the street, rolling over in his mind what might be the connection between the Southerner and Macnee, and what they were cooking up. Pinch face wasn't a gunman of that he was sure. He'd taken a bed at a rooming house not far out of town, between here and the railroad worker encampment. That was a bit of fortuitousness on his part given the task he had in mind before the morning. Anyway, it seemed to him staying at the hotel under Macnee's roof might not be a good idea, more likely to be discovered. Maybe, he spat as he walked, he was being overly cautious. But as a marshal you didn't get a chance making it to a rocking chair by getting sloppy.

Cold, he blew into his exposed hands and prowled around the depot.

He spotted the buckboard hitched to one of the largest draft mules he'd ever seen. It was tied up outside the building as there was no livery out this way. He had his knife out of his boot and set about sawing into the tough hickory wood of the front axle near the wheel. The mule remained calm and quiet. No doubt content from being fed. Despite the temperature, Reeves worked up a sweat and his hand was cramping. He had to stop a few times and massage the muscles. But eventually he was satisfied with his handiwork. After that Reeves wiped his face and returned to the rooming house. He dropped onto his bed with his boots off, clothes and coat on. He napped and after awhile his eyes snapped open. He checked his pocket watch, and was satisfied at the time, a little past 2:30 in the morning. Carrying his boots, he crept down the stairs, avoiding the creaking plank he'd made a note of earlier. At the bottom he put his boots on and slipped out into the dark. He made his way around the gloomy shapes of the workers' tents, a chorus of off-key snoring all around. He got to the area he was looking for, having a good sense of the camp's layout from his survey of it during the daylight.

Here there were clothes and sheets left on the line. It was common for camps of this size for a washer-woman to set up shop and he'd spied the drying items previously. He chanced striking a match and grabbed a pair of workingman's pants and shirt about his size. He blew out the flame and heard a low growl behind him.

"Shit," he cursed softly and turned around to see the shape of a dog near him. The animal regarded him but hadn't advanced or worse, barked yet.

"Here, poochie, here, poochie" he rasped, his words grey wisps in the dark and cold.

The dog remained stationary, an occasional low growl escaping its throat.

Reeves swallowed his fear and stood still too. He put his hands at his sides and waited. His lips were dry and he wetted them with his tongue. Where was a cat when he needed one? The dog strode forward slowly. Reeves resisted the urge to bolt. The dog, a hound mixed with something else he reckoned in the moonlight, started sniffing the air. The canine wasn't particularly big, but large enough to give him trouble. Reeves wondered if there was enough of the scent of the owner on the clean clothes and hopefully he hadn't kicked the dog lately. For several strained moments, the dog circled the man.

The animal eventually sniffed his hand but Reeves knew better than to try and pet him. Deliberately he put one foot in front of the other and, slow as a newborn doe, walked out from among the clothes. The dog trailed after him but broke away at the sound of someone singing,

"I'll take you home again, Kathleen," the voice preened. A relieved Reeves made it back to the rooming house and back in bed, fell directly to sleep.

In the morning he sat on a wooden crate in a corner of the newly-constructed depot's platform. He'd found out when the train was due in and he hoped to blend in, sitting there, doing some whittling, a seemingly idle, maybe injured, worker in his borrowed clothes. He didn't have on the top hat as that was too much of a giveaway. He was not the only completely bald-headed man in town. The train whistled in four minutes ahead of schedule. Out came the telegraph man from inside. There were only two passengers getting off. One was a heavily perfumed woman with a parasol and a feathered hat, and the other was Clayton Goodhew. For sure enough it was the man he'd hoped to see. He was tall, in his fifties, and wore a long coat and thin glasses. He had two pieces of luggage, one of them being a rifle case. In it, Reeves was certain, was his Sharps .50-70. Goodhew, like Crawford, had a reputation as a sharpshooter, a specialist for hire. More, he'd been a regulator for cattlemen associations, range detective, trail guide, a Pinkerton at some point and a bodyguard for a high placed madam in Boston. Whatever Macnee's plan was, he meant to put his intended target or targets in a cross fire from which there would be no escape.

"Mr. Macnee wanted to make sure you go to town fit and proper, Mr. Goodhew," the telegraph man said. "I've got a wagon waiting for you."

"Thank you," the rifleman said, handing his luggage to the other man. The rifle case he held onto as he sparked a flame to his ivory carved pipe.

Reeves quit the depot and hurried back to his room. He got out of the borrowed clothes and into his other wardrobe. He took off for town, leaving the clothes draped over a fence to be found. He didn't hurry and took a more circuitous route back to Three Devils proper. This gave him an opportunity to gain a rise and looking down on the main trail, saw the accident he'd planned. His luck was with him and by golly, the buckboard had snapped the tampered with axle, throwing Goodhew who'd driven it toward town. He lay on the ground, one leg under the buckboard, which lay on its side, the mule casually grazing nearby. Glad the fine animal was unhurt; Reeves reflected as he uttered a phrase in Cherokee and rode on, stern-faced.

Later in Faro Jack's an anxious Macnee checked his pocket watch again and frowned. He told one of his men who had a prominent scar on his cheek, "Go out to the camp and see if that damned train came in."

"Sure thing, boss," the man said and walked out.

Soon the bad news came back to town that Goodhew's leg was broken and he'd be laid up for several weeks. Macnee was a mightily displeased man. The casino owner had been nibbling at a sandwich and seemingly holding his anger in, put it down slowly on his plate and slid it away from him as if he'd lost the taste for food. He rose and announced, "Who can shoot a rifle around here?"

Several voices piped up.

"I mean picking off a target at 150 feet or more, gentlemen."

Three voices spoke this time, Reeves among them.

"Let's get to it," Macnee said.

Soon the three contestants found themselves out behind the livery stable. The man with the barbed wire scar produced a Henry lever action rifle. Sid the barman put empty whiskey and wine bottles atop several haystacks which had been dragged off to the proper distance and set on end.

Reeves had left his preferred Winchester repeater in his room. He knew if he'd brought the weapon with him, that would have raised suspicions that he expected to be using it.

"The targets are placed in such a way as no one can complain about the sun being in their eyes or any other such falderal," Macnee said, smoking a rotund dark cigar and fixing Reeves with an unreadable stare through the smoke. The denizens of the saloon-casino, including Alamosa Bill, and several townspeople had gathered to witness the shooting contest. It wasn't everyday folks got some excitement in the middle of the work-week.

The first one to shoot was an individual with part of his ear lobe missing. He knelt on the ground and shouldered the Henry expertly. He aimed, and sucking in his breath, squeezed off his shots. Each man got five chances. This man blew apart three bottles. There was polite clapping. The second man, balding, stood and, aiming with the Henry, shot and got four out of five. For his effort he received a hearty round of applause.

Reeves stepped up and taking a moment to center himself, cranked off five shots, the Henry fired from shoulder height as the other man had. He too scored four. There was more applause accompanied by murmuring.

"Well, it seems we have a round two," Macnee announced.

More bottles were placed on the hay bales which were pulled back another twenty feet or thereabouts.

The balding man got in position and again he took out four out of five bottles. Reeves shot again, this time firing the rifle like he would his Winchester, from hip level aiming upward, his torso leaning forward as well. And like before, he seemingly struck four out of five bottles as well. He straightened up, displaying a questioning look. He turned to the scarred man. "Would you mind tapping that there green bottle over on the left?"

"What fer?"

"Indulge him, Roscoe," Macnee said, puffing his cigar.

He shrugged and walked over the bottle. He looked at it for a moment then touched the lip. The bottle disassembled into pieces of glass as if it had been held together by an invisible giant's will. There were shouts and clapping.

"Nice work, Ben," said Nat Love, chewing on a wooden match.

Reeves nodded in appreciation. He and the balding man shook hands as Macnee clapped the disguised marshal on the shoulder. "Be at the dry goods store at four today, sharp, understand?"

"Yes, sir."

People begin filing away. Alamosa Bill came over to Reeves who was handing the Henry back to the scarred man who rubbed it down with an oily rag.

"You're might handy there with that piece."

"Thank you." He knew he didn't mean it as a compliment. The other man had a strand of rawhide around his neck tied to the charm Mama Crow had made him.

"You ever shoot more than targets with one?"

"Mister, I can't see that such is a concern of yours."

"Just like to know who I'm working with."

"What's that exactly?"

Alamosa Bill smiled cryptically and walked off, touching the charm underneath his shirt.

Later Reeves knocked on the door of the dry goods store. It was cool under the covered porch and in the store's picture window various items were on display, including colorful bolts of cloth. Reeves idly wondered if he should get swaths of material for his wife. She liked it when he brought home mementoes from the trail to go with the stories he told her of his experiences, often softening some of the harrowing parts. Seems to him such helped to ease the routine she endured taking care of the children and the ranch, even though he hired on seasonal help.

There was a closed sign in the window. Though he couldn't read, Reeves knew the word had more letters than 'open.' Too, the door was locked. The door opened inward by Collette O'Brien.

"Come in, Mr. Jeffers," she said pleasantly.

"Ma'am," he said, touching his hat's brim, hiding his surprise that a woman was in on this meeting. She really was a partner with the Englishman. Inside, she closed and locked the door behind him. Alamosa Bill was there, so were the other hombres he'd previously noted, including the recent Yuma territorial prison resident and the shotgun handling doorman. There was also the scarred man and the pinch-faced ex-Confederate who didn't hide his sourness as he regarded Reeves when he'd entered. Presently there was another knock on the door, and in came Nat Love. This time Reeves allowed his eyebrow to rise.

The other man doffed his hat and said to O'Brien, "Miss Lady."

The gathered sat or leaned on barrels as a standing Carnaby Macnee began. "Except for a couple of you," he waved a hand briefly toward Reeves, "most of you all have some idea why you're here – but until now not when the job was to go down." Being a showman, he paused to let the suspense build. Then, gesturing, he added, "Tomorrow as the cock crows, the silver line will be coming through."

A ripple of excitement coursed through the assembled.

Reeves frowned. He now knew what this was all about but pretended to be in the dark. "Silver line, Mr. Macnee?"

Enjoying the spotlight, Macnee took a deep pull on yet another cigar, drawing out his response. "Some three years ago, your President Grant outlawed the minting of silver coins to appease the banks and the gold trust." Macnee pivoted slightly toward the Southerner, "Making sure those silver deposits the Confederacy had secreted away for another possible insurrection lost their buying power."

The Southerner sat with his arms folded, unmoving.

"Well as it happens," Macnee continued, "Congress in its limited wisdom deemed it necessary to scoop up what silver coinage the federal government could manage and a hefty shipment of these coins will be making their way from where they are in Fort Reno through our new spur here to eventually transfer from the Katy to the Santa Fe on to a smelter in Dallas."

"But what good is taking money you can't spend?" one of the men said.

"You can in Mexico," Macnee said. "In fact I dare say your share will entitle you to live royally." There were blank expressions, that word wasn't understood. "Like kings," he illuminated, sharing a glance with O'Brien.

Now heads bobbed up and down and toothy grins broke out. The man

*"Most of you all have some idea why you're here."*

from Yuma indicated graphically just what he and a couple of senoritas would be doing soon and another man hit him with his hat.

"There's a lady in the room ya, idjit."

"Beggin' your pardon, ma'am." Yuma said.

"I've done worse," she said straight-faced and Yuma got red.

Wryly Macnee intoned, "Let us proceed with the details, shall we?"

After he laid out the scheme Macnee finished with this admonishment. "Everyone sleeps at the hotel tonight and no one goes around alone. I will pair you up and if you don't like it, too jolly bad for you."

Reeves had buzzard's luck and was partnered with Patriss, the Confederate. "You can save it, greyback," Reeves said as soon as the man came toward him, his mouth open to lash out. "I'm not happy about this either. But the good news is, in less than 24 hours, we'll be rid of each other forever. Let's both keep that in mind."

"Fine by me, darkie."

"You can ease up on that too, cracker," Reeves said loud for everyone in the store to hear. "I'm as good with a pistol as I am with a rifle. And I keeps a pig-sticker too."

Patriss turned his head to Macnee who ignored him as he talked with O'Brien.

"Very well," he snarled.

Reeves rode back to the rooming house to fetch his gear and Winchester, trailed by the sulking Southerner. He considered what it meant that Nat Love was also part of this gang. He didn't relish the idea of possibly having to go up against him but maybe it wouldn't come to that. Yet simply getting the drop on Crawford before the robbery went down was going to be nigh impossible given they were now joined at the hip with a shadow. He had no doubts he could overcome the Confederate, but if he did so, that would mean he'd have to make his move fast and try and snatch Crawford who was partnered with the scarred man. That for sure would be pushing his luck he estimated. He might be able to pull it off at dark, but they had to be at Faro Jack's before sundown. Too, he wasn't just a bounty man collecting on his warrants; he was supposed to defend the law as Judge Parker had reminded him more than once. How would it be if he could pull off the grab that he rode away knowing that soldiers would surly die by his inaction?

"No," he muttered, shaking his head, he was going to have to see this through.

"You talking to yerself?"

"Yeah, jus' asking the Lord what I done so wrong to be stuck with your sour puss."

Patriss grumbled, "I was just asking that myself of the one true white Jesus of us all…Ben."

Both rode on in silence, begrudging the other's unwanted company.

Later at the bar and gambling emporium, Reeves played a game of poker. Yuma went upstairs with Big Edna. One of the players announced he was done after losing with three tens. He got up and Nat Love stood near the empty seat.

"Mind if I sit in?" he asked.

"Your money's green," the scarred man said. His name was Mick Clinton.

"Of that I'm sure," Love sat opposite Reeves.

"Jacks or better to open," Clinton said as he dealt the cards.

Reeves was rolling a cigarette.

"I'm out of tobacco, Ben. Could I trouble you for a smoke?"

"My pleasure, Nat." He handed the finished cigarette across.

"Thank you. It's good to be able to depend on your friends, aint it?"

"Mm-hmm," Reeves replied as he rolled another cigarette.

As they played and Reeves wondered if Love was pulling his leg or was being sincere, he noted Patriss and Macnee huddling at one point. The two then left the establishment by the back way. They returned less than half an hour later, wheeling in a wooden packing crate with a hand truck. The crate was wheeled to Macnee's back office.

The following morning, Reeves knew what was in the crate and the role its contents were to play in the robbery. The plan was straight-forward in its ruthlessness and efficiency. The thieves, seven in all including the guard-doorman Claude Moppers, were on their mounts at Corado Pass, a hilly area about a forty minute ride out of Three Devils. This was where the M, K & T tracks met the Santa Fe. The snow had started falling about the time they'd gained the pass and the wooden crate was opened.

"What the hell?" one of the gang said, staring at the contents.

"Hell exactly," the scarred Clinton said, picking up one of the objects. It had a black, rough-hewn surface, long as a brick, though slimmer and with rounded ends. "These here are fancified coal torpedoes; they wuz called in the War." He glared at George Patriss. "You the one that made these."

"That's right."

"George here is what might be termed an expert when it comes to demolition," Macnee said. He was dressed like a dandy's version of a wrangler, complete with a gun, kid gloves and a custom made cartridge belt. "It will be by his hand that we will stop the silver train here. I received word from Tom that the train is on time. I will position you men accordingly and soon we will all be rich as sultans."

Nodding and grinning, the bandits got into place. Patriss and Clinton planted his bombs at specific sections on both sides of the track. The ones originally used in the Civil War were made to look like hunks of coal. In that way they were meant to be mixed in with real coal and shoveled into a ferry's or train's hot box to explode from the heat. Several of the ones they were handling had lengths of fuse to be lit at the right moment. Essentially the idea was to stop the train between the rises of the pass. Crawford would be on one hilltop and Reeves the opposite. As the guards came out of the disrupted train, they were to cut them down. Any left standing who didn't surrender their guns would be dealt with by Macnee and the other gunners, including Nat Love.

Reeves had an alternate plan and it wasn't a good one. But he had no other choice to save innocent lives. The snowing had let up to a light fall and the train's whistle sounded in the near distance. He lay on his stomach on the thin covering of white and sighted down the Winchester's barrel. Up ahead at the curve of the tracks, the sound of the surging locomotive cut through the still air. A curling column of thick black smoke filtered from its unseen smokestack. Crawford too was lying on his stomach, and was also sighting with his Sharps. Reeves slowed his breathing, could feel his heart thump, thump against his chest and in his ears. The train chugged along and calculating his angle, shifted the barrel of his weapon and got off three shots in rapid succession.

"What the hell?" Macnee shouted from hiding as a portion of the tracks blew up with a loud report in the chilly morning. Reeves had noted where the torpedo bombs had been placed and he'd shot at them to cause the explosion. Crawford was shooting at him and one of his rounds went clean through Reeves' hat, missing his brow by a cat's whisker. He fell more than slid down the ridge as more bullets struck the hill above him. He heard the satisfying screech of the train's metal wheels grinding to a halt on the tracks before the pass. Momentarily he was out of sight. But that wasn't going to last.

His goal was to get to a collection of an outcropping of squat rocks at the base of the hill. From there he hoped to hold the others off long enough for the soldiers to arrive from the train. That is if they just didn't reverse course and simply go back the way they'd come. After all, their first priority was to safeguard the silver shipment. Too damn late to worry either way he knew. He was almost at the bottom of the hill as one of the gang, Moppers, came into view, blasting at him with his shotgun.

Reeves flopped backward partly onto his butt and hip as some of the buckshot grazed his lower leg and pinged against the rocks near him. He bit his lower lip due to the stinging pain and returned fire. This caused the other man to seek cover as well. Reeves rolled off the hill and landed hard on his stomach, knocking the wind out of him. Dazed, he sought to clear the dizziness in his head and get his body moving. Getting up was going to be too much effort. He started belly crawling and heard the slight scrape of a boot against brush. Reflexively he rolled onto his back, shooting with the Winchester as he did so. Moppers' blast singed through the air but he was firing his shotgun haphazardly as a death rattle gripped him. He'd stepped out from where he'd hunkered down to get a shot at the lawman. Now Moppers folded in two and sagged to the earth, a surprise frozen on his craggy face.

Reeves' head was clearing and he got to a crouch intending to run to relative safety. But no sooner than he scrambled forward but an explosion went off several yards before him and some of the shrapnel in the thrown torpedo bomb ripped into him. He went over, his hands losing their hold on the rifle. He bled from his upper body and face, though none of the cuts seemed particularly deep. Hands roughly got him to his feet. His ears had a ringing in them.

"Now if you were looking to double cross us, you would have waited until we pulled off the robbery," Macnee observed as the wounded Reeves was held aloft. With no change in his expression, he hit the deputy marshal in the stomach.

"Uggh," Reeves exhaled, hoping his head wouldn't fog again as he also fought down the bile rising in his throat.

"Maybe he's a Pink," Clinton offered.

"Ain't no darkie Pinkertons," one of the others said chidingly. He glanced over at Nat love. "No offense."

Love said nothing.

"Some kind of bounty hunter then," Macnee determined. "Though it's not far-fetched that he might be working directly for a railroad man." He stepped closer to Reeves, regarding him with focused attention like a doctor before surgery. "Is that it, Mr. Jeffers, as that's probably not your name. You working for the railroad itself?"

Reeves remained quiet.

Macnee backhanded him across the jaw. Reeves glowered. "We take him back to town and see what use we can wrangle out of him before I carve out his tongue and his lying eyes. That silver is going to get moved one way or the other and I intend to have it." He turned about, aware of what he'd said. "We all are going to get our cut."

"Damn right," the man from Yuma said.

Hands tied behind his back, a bleeding Bass Reeves was led back to Three Devils on his horse. He had at one point chanced a look at Nat Love but the man gave no indication of anything else on his mind but getting that haul. Coming around the corner of a carriage repair and barrel makers shop at the end of the main street, Love's horse reared up on its two back legs. He circled like that on the horse, the men watching his expertise. As he seemingly got the horse under control, he'd unsheathed his six-shooter and shot the bag of torpedo bombs that had been gathered together again in a canvas sack dangling from George Patriss' saddle. Love blew him and his horse into the next world along with the scarred gunman, Clinton, who'd been riding next to him.

The severed neck and head of Patriss' horse rose end over end through the air. Oddly, the animal had a serene expression. Another robber and his horse that'd also had the misfortune to have been near the now departed Confederate bomb maker were both torn through with numerous ribbons of shrapnel. As he screamed, his horse fell sideways and took out one of the posts supporting the overhang of the barrel maker's porch. In turn the post took out the shop's window. The remaining horses panicked and their riders attempted to get them calmed down in a hurry.

The glass tinkled onto the porch's wood planking and the dirt, and the horse's head struck the Yuma man who took it as a bad omen. As this happened, Love took off after the horse with Reeves on it as its reins had been held by the now deceased Clinton. Macnee had gotten his horse to settle down and he got off shots at Love but he missed. Crawford was using both his hands to rein in his beast that jerked its body around and collided with Macnee who was knocked off his saddle onto the ground.

"Let's git," Love said as he came alongside Reeves and got his hand on the other horse's mane and yanked hard. The horse slowed enough for Reeves to jump onto the back of Love's animal and the two galloped onto a side street and headed toward a passageway between the dry goods store and a feed store.

Reeves yelled over the sound of thudding hoofs, "Not that I'm complaining, but you damn sure cut that close, amigo."

"The only way to play it," Love replied as the two rode into the passageway and dismounted.

The screaming man now whimpered and shivered in the street on his side, next to his dying horse.

Macnee said, "The nearest doctor is half a day's ride." With that, he took the man and mount out of their misery permanently. Thereafter he and the two remaining gun hands rode back to Faro Jack's in silence.

"Now what?" the man from Yuma said.

"Now I get what I'm after," Macnee said between gritted teeth.

Alamosa Bill said nothing.

Inside the saloon and casino, the red-haired Collette O'Brien could tell from their diminished ranks and hands devoid of silver, things hadn't gone as expected. She nodded to Sid the barman and he poured three stiff ones for the men.

Gulping down his second drink, Macnee said, "We got to smoke those two out of there. They only have one horse so there's no hightailing it for them."

"Give it up, Carnaby," Alamosa Bill said. "You don't know the Army isn't right now sending troops in here as they know this here is a wide open town and where better for some owlhoots to nest but here? They know there's no formal law around so they have automatic authority."

The former Yuma inmate said, "He's right. We got to clear out ourselves."

"I'm not going anywhere," Macnee vowed. "Not until my pockets are sufficiently lined, if I might emphasize."

Crawford was pouring himself another drink and slowly sipped from a squat tumbler. He put the glass down quietly, making no noise. "I'm done."

"Then you get nothing, quitter," Macnee sneered.

"Yeah, you keep counting those invisible silver dollars, yer lordship." Crawford touched Mama Crow's charm around his neck. He was alive and unscratched. Far as he was concerned, the damn thing had done its job. Before him on the bar was his Sharps which he'd purposely brought in with him. He turned, the weapon held down at his side. "Me, I know when a job's gone bad. But it ain't like you can't smell the stink, Macnee." His eyes shifted from him to Yuma then back to Macnee. Walking sideways, Crawford exited and took off on his horse. O'Brien watched him ride away through the picture window.

Macnee had a third drink. "Sid, who can you get in town to go up against those two holed up. I'll pay $500 to each man."

"You think that's a good idea, Carnaby?" the woman said, touching his shoulder.

"Even if it's just having the satisfaction of seeing both their ripening corpses, Collette."

The barman observed, "You know as well as me that we got us mostly shopkeepers, drunks and passers through, Carnaby. Now out in the work camp, I figure a few of them roughnecks could be recruited."

"Go do it," he ordered.

Sid shook his head. "They'd want to see you, Carnaby, know the money offer was real. They knew Will not me. Word has probably already reached them about what happened this morning and who knows what's being said out there. Plus they're out laying tracks so they won't be back yet anyhow.

Macnee threw his glass against a wall. "I don't have the luxury of time on my side, Sid. Kind of an urgency right now, old son."

The barman gaped and O'Brien interjected, "I'm afraid he's correct, my dear. At this stage of events, only your presence will assuage doubts. There's bound to be a few hanging around the work camp you can persuade into service."

Macnee stared evenly at her and nodded curtly, "Right as rain as always, my dear." He kissed her quick then said to Yuma, "Stay put and when I get back, we'll fix those two black bastards."

"Sure thing," he said.

Macnee strode out and Big Edna, who'd been cleaning vomit and such off the playing cards with a rag, came over to him. "Why don't you and I pass the time more, constructively?" She pressed her formidable bosom against his chest.

Yuma smiled like a one-eyed cat in a fish cannery. "Yes, ma'am."

They ascended the stairs and O'Brien had a belt of her special Napoleon brandy at the bar. "I'll be right back, Sid," she said and walked outside too. There were a few people in the streets she passed on her way to the feed store where she knew Reeves and Love would be holed up. She walked down the middle of the street, waving her lacy lavender handkerchief.

"Yoo-hoo, Nat, dear, can I have a word?"

Inside the store, the storekeeper bound in the back, Reeves looked from the window he was stationed below with his rifle to Love. "Nat, dear?" He rested an elbow on one of the burlap sacks of grain he'd stacked up as well for protection.

"Me and Collette go back a ways," he replied taciturnly.

"Maybe it's a trap."

"Maybe." Love stepped to the door and cracked it open a sliver, glancing about. "Come on, Collie."

She entered and told them what Carnaby was up to.

Confused, Reeves pondered aloud, "Why you throwing your lot in with us?"

Hand on her hip she gave him a lopsided grin. "I'm not throwing in with both of you."

Then Reeves understood. He pointed at Love. The woman had an arm around his waist. "Oh, you two, you two all along…" He rubbed a hand on the back of his neck. "I'll be hornswaggled." He snapped his fingers. "Where are Crawford and Yuma now?"

"I got Big Edna keeping Yuma occupied. The other one you mentioned, he took off heading west less than half an hour ago."

Reeves said, "Let's get set for Macnee and whoever else he comes back to town with. Then I can take off for Alamosa Bill."

Love said, "You can head out now, Bass. We got this covered. Anyway, I see it as you lookin' out for my end too."

"You sure?"

"Yep."

"You know I'll square it up with you, Nat, when I come out on the other side of this."

"I know."

Love gave Reeves his horse and the deputy marshal headed west as well. Nat hadn't just been stopping in town after a cattle drive. He and that redhead planned to rob the robbers or at least Carnaby all along. But why had Love stuck his neck out saving him? Out of friendship or business? Did Nat Love do some ciphering and concluded that an alive Reeves meant a possibility that Crawford would be taken in for that big bounty fee? Since the silver heist had gone bust, he might have seen there was still a chance at some money in all this deal, knowing Reeves would cut him in for a share given all he'd done.

Well, he told himself, settling in the saddle, no sense worrying over what was as he had best be focused on what needed doing. Reeves made a "snick" sound, lightly tapped the sides of the horse with his boots, and rode determined out of Three Devils.

Carnaby Macnee left the mess hall having secured the services of one of the men in there eating an early lunch. He was crossing over to the telegraph office at the temporary train depot when the lady of the evening Brandyrose stepped out from behind a tent and put two bullets from of her Navy Colt into his brain pan. He flopped forward face down on the wood planking, instantly expired. Later she'd find out the Army had identified him as the ringleader of the attempted silver robbery and had issued a thousand dollar bounty on his head. She'd shot him because she'd overheard why he was in camp and she saw this as her opportunity to get back at him for throwing her over for that Collette. Brandyrose collected the bounty, moved back east and was able to start her life over.

Less than two days later out on the trail as a heavy snowfall began that night, Bass Reeves got the drop on William Crawford, also known as Alamosa Bill, where he was camped out amid a pine grove. The rawhide around his neck had chaffed him some and he'd only a minute before placed the charm Mama Crow had prepared for him on a nearby branch heavy in a white coating. Reeves waited until morning and under a clear, cold sky of steel gray, took his prisoner directly back to Fort Smith federal prison. It was called Hell on the Border by its inmates, and they did not mean this affectionately.

THE END

# From Peckinpah to Leonard

Gil Westrum, "Pardner, do you know what's on the back of a poor man when he dies? The clothes of pride. And they're not a bit warmer to him than when he was alive."

That line is from Sam Peckinpah's second film, *Ride the High Country* written by N.B. Stone (and William S. Roberts and Peckinpah himself according to some sources) and perfectly sums up the flawed, antihero Westrum veteran cowpoke actor-producer Randolph Scott played. The same film that contained the often repeated, "I want to enter my house justified," which is a variant on a verse from Luke in the Bible – a line that inspired the title of the modern day marshal cable show, *Justified*, based on characters by the late wordsmith Elmore Leonard.

From Peckinpah's films to Leonard's novels like *Valdez is Coming*, all those *Have Gun Will Travel* episodes I've re-watched several times since seeing them with my dad as a little kid; Marvel's western comics like the *Rawhide Kid* and *Gunhawks*; *Kung Fu*, the Apache paperback vigilante series (written by two Britishers) to *El Dorado* onto *Django Unchained*, the western has always been a genre I've enjoyed. But it wasn't a genre I'd written in much.

Still there was no way not to do a Bass Reeves story when the opportunity arose. He was a frontier marshal of the badlands, a real figure who cut a hell of a swath in the Wild West. His exploits are the stuff of legend. Yet as that opening line suggests, I knew I wanted a plot that had some twists to it. If Bass is in the lineage of Joel McCrea's upright Steve Judd in *Ride the High Country*, I needed my Westrum. Well, I have him in the form of Nat — pronounced "Nate" — Love, who is also based on a historic figure. Though I freely admit I took several liberties in the name of artistic license with him in his role in "Ride from Three Devils."

Me, I had a great time writing my story and I hope the reader enjoys its telling, and the three other stories in this sure to be acclaimed collection.

**GARY PHILLIPS** - Born under a bad sign with family roots in Texas near the Guadalupe River and the Mississippi Delta, Phillips must keep writing to forestall his appointment at the crossroads. Recent work includes co-editing and contributing to the sci-fi anthology *Occupied Earth*, stories about life and resistance under the alien bootheels of the Mahk-Ra; co-writer of *Peepland*, a gritty comics miniseries set in '80s New York coming from Titan Comics; and a reviewer said of his collection of edgy superhero tales *Astonishing Heroes*, "It's a book for anyone who remains nostalgic for the golden age of Toei films, blaxploitation movies, and lusty grindhouse cinema." Please visit his website at: gdphillips.com.

# Whiskey Road

by Mel Odom

Working by lantern light in pouring rain, Bass Reeves stood shoulder deep in an outlaw's grave long after sunset. He pushed the shovel home in the red clay that covered the rough wooden casket and cussed himself.

"Ain't nothin' that couldn't have waited till the light of day, Baz." He'd told himself that a few times now, but it hadn't stopped him from coming into the old graveyard and setting to the task. Curiosity chafed him most times. "And it's a good thing you don't believe in ha'nts."

Rain dripped steadily from the brim of his hat, and occasional drops crept under his rain slicker, touching him with the unseasonable chill that sometimes came in the Indian Territories during April. Heaving the soaked earth over his shoulder onto the pile he'd made at the side of the grave, he was wishful of being back home in Arkansas. He'd been on the trail for a while this time out.

The noise of his children, all of them carrying on about something, would have filled the home to bursting. But he would have had the quiet of the horse barns. And he preferred the smell of fresh hay and healthy horses over the grave stink that clung to this miserable hole in the muddy ground.

*Thunk!*

The shovel handle vibrated in Bass's callused hands when the blade bit into the wooden box.

"There you are, Muskrat." Bass smiled in the darkness, figuring he was only a short while away from a warm, dry bed in the local hotel. "If that is you in this box. When I fetch you up outta here, guess we'll know soon enough."

Inspired by his success, Bass reached up and moved the coal oil lantern hanging from the plain wooden cross over the grave. Pale yellow light fell into the hole. Leaning into the job at hand, listening to the steady *plop-plop-plop* of the rain hitting his hat and slicker, he cleared away the last layer of red clay between him and his prize.

When the rough wood lay naked under his boots, Bass tossed the shovel out of the grave and reached up for the rope he'd brought to haul out the coffin.

A shadow stepped out of the darkness beside the spreading blackjack tree that had kept Elton "Muskrat" Mater company for the last six months. Lightning flared across the sky, revealing the maelstrom of dark clouds that obscured the slivered moon.

The flare burned bright across the nickel-plated short barrel of the Smith & Wesson Safety Hammerless .38 revolver only inches from Bass's face. The pistol was new, a double-action piece some folks called the "Lemon Squeezer" because a man could keep on pulling the trigger till all five rounds fired.

"Go for them guns you're wearing and I'm gonna shoot out your eyes." The speaker was a short, lean man wearing a derby and a slicker and a week's growth of whiskers.

Bass gripped the coiled rope and placed his other hand on the mud. "I ain't gonna reach for 'em."

The man's smile showed in the lantern glow. He was in his early thirties, almost twenty years younger than Bass, nearly a foot shorter than Bass's six feet two inches, and at least fifty pounds lighter than Bass's hundred and ninety. A horseshoe-shaped scar on the man's right cheek pulled at his mouth, fitting him with a permanent leer.

In the darkness, Bass couldn't see the man's hair, but he was wagering it was the color of beaten gold. He looked up at the man affably. "I'm betting you're Shoofly Bierstadt."

"You're a mite too inquisitive already, ain't you? Poking around in a dead man's grave ain't something a cautious man would be about, now is it?"

The Pennsylvanian Dutch accent had all but gone away. However, Bass had a keen ear for intonations and speech patterns.

Bass grinned. "Yep, you're Shoofly. Your momma and daddy named you Albrecht, but once you and your younger brother up and left them after killin' that young lady you set your cap for, you went by Shoofly. Then you and your brother—what was his name?"

"Kartner, you hulking brute. His name was Kartner. And you killed him."

"I did." Bass worked at being agreeable. "Ol' Kartner cut up a Choctaw girl down to Tushka Homma last year. Guess he learned cowardly killin' from you. Murderin' that girl made him feel like he was somethin', I reckon. I got a writ for him from Judge Parker and come on down to fetch him.

Found him, too. Told him I'd bring him back to Fort Smith and see him swing for what he done. Likely he didn't care to have his neck stretched, so he went for his pistol and I went for mine, and—well, that's all she wrote. Maybe he was faster with that knife he used on that poor girl."

Shoofly's face turned hard and brittle.

"I seen to it he got planted right proper in Tushka Homma. Maybe you seen his grave? Lemme know what you think. I thought it was a good spot. Shady in the heat of the day, and not a water trap like this grave." Bass tapped his shovel against the muddy grave box. "I waited around a few days to see if you would come callin', but you didn't and I had other things I had to get to."

"Shut up, you black beast!"

Bass let the name calling pass him by. In the long run, the slurs meant nothing. They weren't like a man using his fists or a gun. "I saw you in the bar tonight." Bass had stopped off at the bar long enough to get a hot meal and directions to the cemetery. He'd waited around for the rain to break, or to decide if he could just wait till morning to dig into his latest assignment.

The rain hadn't let up and his curiosity had won out. One of these days it might just get him killed. Maybe even tonight.

"You saw me and you just ignored me?" Shoofly scowled.

"No. I don't have no paper on you. I woulda telegraphed the judge's office in the morning, squared it away and got a writ. I wasn't gonna forget about you. You and your brother robbed a few folks here in the Territories."

"Looks like there's enough room in that grave for one more." Shoofly grinned and pointed the pistol at Bass. "You got all the work done an' I don't think the present occupant will object to double-bunking."

Forcing himself to keep smiling and to ignore the gun in his face, Bass shook his head. "Now do you really think I come out here by myself?"

Shoofly didn't glance around. "I ain't falling for that."

"Didn't think you would." Exploding into motion, Bass ducked his head to his right and swept up the coiled rope in his left hand. The pistol went off, blurring his vision with the muzzle flash and splitting the quiet hanging over the graveyard with the detonation.

Knowing he'd missed death by inches, if that much, Bass looped the rope over Shoofly's gunhand, set his boots in the grave, and yanked hard. His opponent screamed as he flew from his perch and toppled into the dark hole.

Scrambling to press his back against the muddy side of the grave, Shoofly tried to bring his pistol to bear again. Bass closed one of his big hands over the killer's gunhand, covering Shoofly's hand and the back of the revolver. The outlaw managed to shoot again and the bullet tore into the mud wall behind Bass. Almost as sudden, the United States Deputy Marshal backhanded his opponent in the face. Shoofly flew backward and settled on his rump on the coffin in a loose-limbed sprawl against the other end of the grave.

All the fight left with Shoofly's consciousness. Blood leaked from his cheek where his flesh had split from the impact. Even for a man his size, Bass had big hands, hardened through years of use.

A shadow fell into the grave.

Not wishful of any further surprises, Bass drew one of the Colt Model P .44 revolvers that hung in crossed belts at his waist. He eared back the hammer and readied himself to fire from the hip.

"Everything okay down there?" Alfred Tubby peered down into the grave. He held his Winchester rifle at the ready. He was mostly Cherokee Indian, but he had some white in him too. His hatchet face and long black hair offered mute testimony to his Indian roots, but his hazel eyes guaranteed he wasn't full blood. Strands of gray showed in his hair and his face looked weathered these days. He wore jeans, boots, a cotton shirt, and a slicker that covered him better than the one Bass wore covered him.

Even though the marshal was almost fifty, Bass knew Alfred had twenty years on him. Still, the old man was spry and mean as a he-coon.

Growling a curse, Bass leathered his Colt. "I should shoot you. Sneaking up on me in the dark, it's a wonder I *didn't* shoot you."

"I knew you wouldn't shoot me."

"Well, you're the only one of us who did."

"And I didn't sneak up on you. I'm Indian. I can't help it if I move quiet." Alfred nodded at the unconscious man. "Who's your friend?"

"He's not a friend. He's a payday. His name's Bierstadt. Did he come alone?"

"Yes. I hung back to make sure."

"You watched him come into the cemetery?"

"Yeah."

Puzzled irritation flared through Bass. "Why didn't you stop him?"

"I thought maybe he was a man coming to pay his respects."

"At this time of night? In this rain?"

"People who are grieving, they have strange ways. And some days I can't make no sense of white men at all." Alfred pointed at the coffin under Bass's boots. "You haven't finished uncovering that?"

"Does it look like I have?"

"It might be best if you get to it. Before anybody else decides to come calling."

"Now who would do that?"

Cradling his rifle with one arm, Alfred gestured to the graveyard with the other. "Some of these folks around us might get tired of lying there and decide to get up to stretch their legs."

Although he didn't believe in ghosts and wasn't at all sure about the afterlife being the way the Bible thumpers liked to describe it with streets of gold and such, the suggestion that the dead might rise bothered Bass a mite more than he was willing to let on. Even the dead might not care for drowning.

"You could help." Bass adjusted his hat.

"Not me. Somebody has to watch over you."

"I hope you do better with the next ambusher."

Alfred waved off the complaint with a loose hand and kept walking across the graveyard. Somewhere under the nearby trees, their horses nickered.

Bass reached down and frisked Shoofly, finding a long-bladed folding knife and a set of brass knuckles in the man's pockets. Bass used piggin strings from his back pocket to tie the man's hands behind his back. Then he grabbed hold of the man's shirt and belt and heaved Shoofly out of the grave. The unconscious man landed atop the pile of grave mud with a squelch.

"Well? Is that the Muskrat fella?" Alfred stood a few feet behind Bass.

The deputy held his lantern close to the dead man's sunken face. The body was shriveled up like an old apple, spotted with decomposition, and looked brittle. The beetles and other burrowing insects had been at him some, but he still looked passably human in the ill-fitting black suit. The problem was, what was left of him didn't look enough like Elton Mater for Bass.

"You want to take a look at him? Tell me what you think?" Bass offered the lantern.

"Not me. From what I can see from over here, he looks worse for the wear."

"You afraid he's gonna get up out of this coffin and get you?" Bass couldn't help needling his posseman. They'd traveled together now and again, and he liked the old man.

Alfred shot him a reproachful look. "Maybe you like it out here in the rain with all these dead folks. Not me. I don't like disturbin' them."

Shaking his head, Bass replaced the cover on the casket and hammered the nails back into place with a gloved fist. "This ain't Muskrat. Don't know who it is."

"So Muskrat's still out there."

"Not for long. I mean to find him and fetch him to hang from a Fort Smith gallows at Judge Parker's pleasure." Bass strode across the cemetery, avoiding looking at the wooden crosses and the stone markers. He tried not to think of what now slept under them.

The horses whickered as he neared them. He and Alfred had brought a wagon in case Bass needed to return the body to Stringtown proper. Now that he knew what he knew, he wanted to have a word with the Choctaw Lighthorseman in the area.

If the tip about the wrong man being buried in Muskrat's grave was now verified, it meant that the little boy who had gone missing was in a mess of trouble.

"Why'd you bring him here?" Standing beside the wagon, Choctaw Lighthorseman Robert Little held up a lantern to better view the dead man in the muddy coffin.

"Because the man at the hotel would charge me double if I took him there. Why do you think?" Bass stood there in the alley in back of a mercantile where the Choctaw Lighthorse Police unit maintained an office. He was drenched and wanted nothing more than a hot bath and a dry bed.

Little was in his forties and had been keeping the peace for over twenty years. His face was haggard and jowly, framed a little by a wispy beard. He was full blood Choctaw. Bass had heard of the man and knew him to be good at his job, but nobody wanted to work at night. Or in the rain. Especially on a corpse.

"Couldn't you have just left him there where you found him?"

"No." Bass worked at being patient. He was good with people. That was one of the reasons Judge Parker had made him a deputy marshal representing his court.

"After you found out he wasn't this Muskrat guy, you didn't need him no more." Little took his light away from the dead man. Rain hissed and popped on the lantern's heated hurricane glass.

"I don't need him anymore, but you do."

"No, I don't."

"Somewhere out there, you got somebody that knows this man didn't come home. You need to let them know where he is."

"He looks white to me." Little glanced at Alfred, who leaned against the office's back wall out of the rain. The old man kept his rifle in his arms. "Don't he look white to you?"

Irritated, Bass snorted. "He looks white because the blood's drained out of his face. He's Indian."

Little cussed, but he didn't have his heart in it. He was stuck with the body and he knew it, but he had to try getting rid of it one more time. "That means you're looking for Muskrat for murdering this man. You'll need the body as evidence."

"This man wasn't murdered." Bass took Little's lantern and shone it onto the dead man's face. Rain crawled along the pallid, waxy features pockmarked by insect predation.

"Man's got a bullet hole between his eyes."

"He was shot after he was dead." Bass traced a forefinger along the side of the dead man's face. "You see how this side of his face is darker than the other?"

Little leaned in a mite closer. "So?"

"Means he died while he was lying on his side. Given the jaundiced coloration too, I'd say he gave up the ghost on account of alcohol poisoning. Either too much whiskey or he got him a bad batch. Then Muskrat and his boys found him and decided to make it look like them Pinkerton detectives killed him during that robbery on the Katy line six months back."

The Katy was the Missouri-Kansas-Texas Railroad that ran north and south alongside Stringtown. The town had grown up along the tracks, but it had originally been named Springtown because of the natural springs in the hill country.

According to the reports the Pinkertons had filed, they'd engaged the train robbers and managed to kill Muskrat. One of the detectives claimed the kill, said he saw Muskrat go down and other outlaws throw his body on a horse. The gang made off with the cashbox and pursuit followed. Only hours later, Muskrat's body was abandoned in the woods.

"This dead man was identified as Muskrat." Little looked up at Bass. "You saying somebody made a mistake?"

"Read them reports about the robbery." Bass closed the coffin. "Says that Muskrat was identified by Pete Whitfield, a man known to associate with the gang but not wanted for anything. I reckon Whitfield was paid off to make the false identification. If I was you…"

"You ain't." Little was determined to hang onto his obnoxiousness.

"…I'd find Whitfield and start asking questions." Bass smiled, ignoring the man's belligerence. He couldn't blame Little. Getting a muddy corpse brought out in the middle of the night was disconcerting. "Like you pointed out, I ain't you, but I bet your boss will point you in that direction too."

"Do you know how much gone a man can be in six months?"

"Whitfield's out there. All them bad men are out there. They love it in the Territories. Till they get caught and go before Judge Parker." Bass touched his fingers to his hat brim. "I'll leave you with this one. Take the wagon back to the stable when you can. I'll let the liveryman know where it is." He pointed to Shoofly, who lay curled up unconscious next to the coffin. "Hold onto that one for me till I get back. He's wanted for trying to kill a deputy marshal."

"How long is that gonna be?"

"Long as it takes. I'll let you know." Bass untied his tall sorrel from the back of the wagon. The horse stood there partially covered by the tarp that protected Bass's saddle and equipment, but the animal still looked mighty miserable.

"Gonna charge you room and board for your prisoner."

"See to it you keep him alive." Instead of mounting the sorrel, Bass led his mount toward the Stringtown Hotel while Alfred trailed after with his own mount.

During the walk through the muddy street scored by wagon wheel ruts, Bass kept wondering why anyone would try to fake Muskrat's death and how that tied into the boy's disappearance.

And to the murder of the young woman, Honeysuckle Paul.

"I knew her." Glenn Hefferran, one of Stringtown's morticians, looked down at the dead woman lying on his office table.

The room was hardly big enough to call an office, it being big enough to hold the examination table and the corpse with some walking around room on all sides. Cabinets held supplies that he used in his trade, and Bass was familiar with most of them due to his long peacekeeping career.

The deceased woman was nineteen according to the papers Hefferran had on her, and she had been pretty enough to turn heads. Her long black hair would have hung down to her waist if she'd been standing. The gray pallor had drained her of most of her color and robbed her of some of her beauty, but the high cheekbones and wide-spaced eyes remained.

"Knowing them makes it harder." Bass leaned down and inspected the knife wound in the left side of the dead woman's neck. He made no effort to remove the sheet that protected her modesty. "Just the one wound?"

"Yeah." Hefferran was short and heavy, making negotiating space in the room somewhat challenging. He wore glasses and slicked his hair down. He looked like he was in his late thirties, but he could have been older. A heavy linen smock protected the suit he wore.

Bass traced the short cut with his forefinger about an inch from the dead girl's skin. "No hesitation marks. The killer knew what he was doing. Just slipped in and sliced her carotid, then let her bleed out."

"Death came quick. No more than minutes." Hefferran's voice got tight. "After the initial puncture, she didn't feel any pain. Just drained away."

"Man who did this had him some experience cutting throats."

"He could have learned on livestock."

"Butchering a cow is different than cutting a man. Remember when you cut into your first body? The feel of the flesh peeling back from the blade?"

"I do."

"Did you cut a straight line like this?"

Hefferran shook his head and released a breath. "It was a hard thing."

Bass nodded. A man remembered such things. "It ain't something you do the first time perfect. Unless you've had some practice."

"I suppose not."

Straightening, taking a step around the body, Bass looked at the dead woman from a fresh angle. He hated seeing dead so young and it bothered him that he didn't feel the remorse as badly as he used to. Something in him had dulled, grown callused. But the desire to catch men who did such things had only grown sharper. "Any bruises?"

Hefferran lifted the sheet to reveal bruising along the dead woman's right forearm. The marks left by four fingers and a thumb showed plain enough.

Lowering his hand to within inches of the pallid skin, Bass took measure of the bruises. "Big man did this."

"I'd say so."

"No other marks?"

"None."

Bass ran his fingers through his thick mustache as he pictured the events in his mind. "Her killer grabbed her and stuck her. She got close enough for him to do that. Means she knew him, trusted him. At least, she did before he murdered her." He cut his gaze over to the mortician. "They say she had her son with her when she was killed. Little boy named Nate."

"Nathan, I think his given name is."

"Where's his daddy?"

"You'd have to talk to the family about that. As far as I know, there is no father."

"Can't be true. You have a child, you have a momma and a daddy. Always a pair."

"You'll have to talk to Mrs. Paul about that."

"I will. Thank you for your time."

After getting directions to the Paul place from the Lighthorseman lieutenant manning the desk that morning, and checking in on Shoofly, who was not impressed with his accommodations, Bass rode down to the telegraph office. The gray-faced building sat in back of the railroad tracks that ran through the town. A sign above the door advertised messenging services.

Alfred sat on a wooden bench out front with a newspaper in his hands. Bass didn't know which paper it was, but he knew the Cherokee and the Choctaw set a lot of store by the printed page.

Bass nodded to his postman; took off his hat, and entered the telegraph office.

A balding man sat behind a high desk. A green visor shadowed his eyes and a thin mustache crawled along his upper lip below a pointed nose.

"May I help you?" the man asked.

"I need to send a telegram to Fort Smith, care of Judge Parker."

The clerk picked up a pencil and a small pad and pushed them over to Bass. "Just write what you want sent and I'll see to it."

Still feeling that old embarrassment at not being able to read or write, Bass pushed the pad back to the clerk. "If I write it, you ain't gonna be able to read it. Might be best if you take it down."

"All right." The clerk picked up the pencil. "Go ahead."

Hon Frank Boles
Dear Sir
Please reissue the writ for Elton Mater, also known as Muskrat, who is guilty of train robbery. Have opened the Stringtown grave and it ain't him. Am tracking down leads about the missing boy and those who took him today. I will keep you informed.

Yours truly,
Bass Reeves

After the clerk finished writing on the pad, he offered it up to Bass for inspection. "Will that do it?"

Bass stared at the jumble of letters and wished he could pick out the words. He'd grown up a slave, and by the time he'd lit out for the Indian Territories with hounds on his heels, he'd never had time to learn.

"Yeah." He nodded. "That'll do. There'll be a quick response. I'll be out front when it gets here." He paid for the telegram, then went back to the porch and took a seat to wait.

Frank Boles managed the judge's office and legal affairs, and he wasn't a man to let grass grow. Alfred kept himself busy with his paper while Bass watched a stagecoach go by, probably headed for the Texas Trail. Farther out, the locomotive sitting in front of the train station blew a cloud of smoke and steam, gave two ear-splitting whistle blasts, and chugged into motion, snorting and snarling like some mechanical bull.

Bass felt like the pulling engine. Now that the writ had been sent for, he was getting up a head of steam too. It might be too late for the momma, but he was determined to save her little boy and bring him home to his family safe.

Just before noon, Bass reined in the sorrel and sat gazing at the old house tucked into a copse of trees that seemed bent on absorbing the structure back into the scrub forest surrounding it. The clapboards showed gray, untouched by paint and fiercely weathered by age and the harsh climate. The windows were snipers' crosses running vertical and horizontal a few inches each way, meant for defense and not for letting the sun in. This was a place where folks hunkered down to survive, not live.

Bass had built his own house, a fine eight bedroom structure, and he'd put pride in every stone and piece of timber he'd used. His wife and kids deserved the best he could give them, and he'd given it.

The people who lived in this house had come during hard times and kept them tucked in bed with them ever since. The death of Honeysuckle Paul and the theft of her child was just insult piled on top of injury.

A small barn sat to the east and one of the doors hung slightly ajar. The tiny corral was next to a pigpen where a few hogs rooted in the black earth. A henhouse sat a short distance away. The overgrown grass in the yard stood tall, not beaten down like it would be under heavy foot traffic. The Pauls didn't see much in the way of visitors.

Alfred sat with crossed hands on his saddle pommel while his paint pony chewed grass. "This is a lonesome place."

Bass nodded. "It is that." He put his heels to the sorrel's sides and moved forward.

When he was within a hundred feet of the house, a branch dropped from a nearby tree, then a gunshot rang out, splitting the silence and scaring birds in nearby trees into flight.

"That's far enough," a woman's voice bellowed.

Before Bass could respond, a second bullet slapped into the rain-softened ground and ripped a furrow only an arm's length away. As the *crack* of the shot rolled over him, he reined in quick. The horse danced in momentary fear. He held both hands up at his shoulders.

"Hold your fire! I'm a United States Deputy Marshal and this is my posseman. I'm here about the death of Miss Honeysuckle Paul. I'm supposed to talk to Mrs. Lucisa Paul. She sent a letter to Judge Isaac Parker about her granddaughter's murder and her great-grandson's kidnappin'."

For a moment, the silence returned, interrupted only by the twittering of birds alighting once more in the branches overhead. Then a woman's voice called out. "Let me see your badge."

Gingerly, Bass slid his coat over so the star pinned to the left side of his chest showed. He tried not to think that the silver pinwheel with the cutout star was just a good target. "I'm Deputy Marshal Bass Reeves. You folks should have gotten a letter that I'd be by."

Women's voices sounded for a moment, then an older woman's voice responded. "Come ahead, Marshal. My granddaughter is a mite skittish these days, what with everything that's gone on."

"Thank you, ma'am." Bass slowly lowered his hands and urged the sorrel forward again. "I purely don't want to be shot by mistake this morning."

"You didn't get missed by mistake," the young woman said. "If you get shot by me, it's because I intended to shoot you."

Bass smiled, liking the fire in the woman's voice. "That's good to know, ma'am."

Reaching the lopsided porch, Bass stepped down from the saddle. He wrapped the sorrel's reins around a porch support and hoped the horse didn't step back and pull the leaning roof down.

Alfred tied up the paint at the other end of the porch, giving them about ten feet of separation. The woman would have to be really good to get them both if that was what she was of a mind to do.

A young woman carrying a Henry Yellowboy .44 rifle stepped out onto the porch. She didn't aim the weapon at Bass, but it wouldn't have taken much to raise it into position.

She was short and slim and hard, like a hank of rawhide fitted into worn jeans and a man's shirt that had been remade to fit her better. The shirt had been dark blue once upon a time, but it had faded from wear and washing. Her short dark hair barely hung to her jaw in a line that showed enough irregularity to advertise she'd done the cutting herself. Her brown eyes were tight and mean, cold as ice.

Holding his hands out to his sides, knowing Alfred wouldn't move into the line of fire, Bass smiled up at the young woman. "I'm not feeling particularly invited."

The young woman didn't say anything.

"Rose!" the old woman's voice called from within. "Step aside and let the marshal in. I sent for help, and I mean to have it."

"We don't need no help, Granny." Despite her protestations, Rose let the rifle barrel drop alongside her leg. "I told you I would take care of getting Nate back to home."

"I ain't gonna lose another granddaughter to those men. Now, please, mind your granny."

Reluctantly, staring daggers, Rose retreated inside the house but didn't turn her back.

Doffing his hat, Bass followed the young woman into the house, seeming to fill up the small room all by his ownself. Alfred waited outside, minding the horses. They didn't make a habit of being in the same spot when times were uncertain.

In her early seventies at least, the old woman sat looking whipcord tough in a rocking chair to one side of the fireplace. She wore a long brown dress that reached to her ankles and wore her long gray hair in a braid. Her Indian blood showed in her high cheekbones and bronze skin. Glasses made her dark eyes big in a pinched face. A .44 Dragoon pistol sat on a small table to her right.

*A young woman carrying a Henry Yellowboy .44 rifle stepped out.*

"Well," the old woman said, "I guess they sent a marshal big enough to get the job done."

In spite of the tension in the room, Bass couldn't help but smile. "I surely hope so, ma'am. You are Mrs. Lucisa Paul?"

"I am ever since I married my mister, may he rest in peace."

Bass aimed his hat at a nearby chair. "Might I sit?"

"Light and let's talk a spell."

"First of all," Bass said once he'd taken the offered seat, "I'd like to offer you my condolences regardin' your granddaughter."

"I appreciate your kindness, Marshal, but we can't go tending to the dead, now can we?" Lucisa's voice was hard, but there was some brittleness to it. She was tough, but losing her granddaughter and great-grandson weighed on her. "They've gone on ahead. It's the livin' that needs tendin'."

Bass held his hat in both hands between his knees. "Yes, ma'am, I reckon that's so."

"God knows our family ain't had no shortage of death since we been in this holler. At this point, I'm more concerned about my great-grandson." The old woman's voice quavered a little at that, but she firmed up her chin and looked hard at Bass, as if daring him to fault her.

"Do you know who took him?" Bass asked.

"Not for a fact, but I've got a notion."

"In your letter you said you believe your great-grandson is in the hands of Elton Mater."

"Muskrat, that's right." Lucisa studied Bass. "You went and looked into that grave before you come here, didn't you?"

Bass made it a point to never lie. No matter how unappealing, the truth was always best. "Yes, ma'am, I did."

"Checking out my story."

"Yes, ma'am. Elton Mater was reported dead. I needed to check on things."

"Did you find Muskrat's body?"

"No, ma'am. That body belonged to someone else."

The old woman cursed, and she could blister a blue streak. "I knew that devil's death was too good to hope for. I told my girls he wouldn't have died so sudden or so easy. I suspicioned he faked his death."

"Why?"

"Because of the convenience! Him and his men rob a train and get away, but they ride off with him shot between the eyes? No sir, I never bought that."

"Then why did you wait six months before sending that letter?"

"Because my granddaughter was still alive and that baby still lived in this house. Where he's *supposed* to be. Until he was took a few days ago." Her voice cracked, and for the first time Bass saw the frailty in the old woman.

He gave her a moment to take control of herself. "Do you think Muskrat killed your granddaughter?"

"Maybe." She waved a hand. "I don't know. What I do know is this: about three years ago, Honeysuckle took up with one of Muskrat's men while they were hanging around Stringtown." She smoothed her dress over her thighs. "Honeysuckle weren't no bad girl. She was a good 'un. Just had a heart too big, that's all. She got sweet on that no-account, got her head turned by his handsome looks. She told me and Rose how she thought she could get him out of the outlaw life and away from Mater. Said that man didn't belong on the owlhoot trail because he was too fine and cultured. Instead, what she got was Nate after that man rode off and left her." Her rheumy eyes misted. "Nate's a little angel, Marshal. Just a baby."

"Yes, ma'am. I've got children of my own. Ain't nothin' finer than little ones."

She nodded and wiped away a lone tear that tracked down her leathery cheek. "Children is a blessin' an' a hardship."

"Yes, ma'am, but even both ways we're better for 'em."

She met his eyes with hers, and there wasn't an inch of backup in her when she did. "If I was younger and still able, I'd go after that man what took Nate. An' I'd nail his hide to the barn door." She sipped her breath. "I come from pioneer stock. Trouble an' hard times wasn't nothin' but a part of the day between breakfast an' supper. But I *ain't* the woman I used to be. So I'm countin' on you."

"I'll do right by you, Mrs. Paul."

"See that you do."

"If you don't mind me movin' things along, I don't think you had me ride out here just to talk about the past. Was it Mater that took your grandbaby?"

"Not him. I knew Mater still bein' alive would interest you an' Judge Parker. But this has to do with Mater. The man who took Nate was ridin' with Mater. Probably still is. Me, I got to thinkin' we were all well shut of them outlaws, that everythin' was gonna be okay. Until Honeysuckle ran into one of Mater's men in the mercantile a couple weeks ago."

"Not Nate's daddy?"

"No." Lucisa cursed again. "An' that man ain't a daddy."

"I'm gettin' a little lost as to how this all came about," Bass admitted. "You say your daughter met one of Mater's cronies a couple weeks back?"

"Yes."

"Did she mention a name?"

Lucisa glanced at Rose.

"His name was Pete." Rose held her arms crossed and looked even angrier than before. She acted like giving up the name was as bad as hammering her thumb.

"Pete Welker?" Bass remembered the name from what he remembered about Mater. "Some folks call him Piebald."

Rose shrugged. "Pete was all I was told."

"The reason they call him Piebald is because his hair and beard are two different colors. His hair's gray, turned early, but his beard's black as coal."

Lucisa narrowed her gaze at her granddaughter. "Is that the man?"

Rose gritted her teeth for a moment and didn't look at her mother. "Honeysuckle saw him, wasn't me."

"Your sister ain't here to ask, Rose Marie Paul, so I'm askin' you 'cause I don't rightly remember an' you got a better memory than I do."

Not wanting the two women to unleash the fight that threatened to boil over between them, Bass shifted his boots, thumping them against the floor just enough to get their attention. He knew how things between women could get from watching his wife and their daughters go at each other. Being between them wasn't a place a sane man wanted to be.

"Ain't nobody else ridin' with Mater goin' by the name of Pete. So what happened when your girl seen this man?"

"They talked some." Lucisa frowned. "'Course I didn't know about it until this one told me later. Them two girls, they was thick as thieves. Kept their secrets."

Bass knew how kids could be. When they weren't watched closely enough, they got away with living in their own worlds, had their own rules for things. Bass kept his kids busy with chores and school work, but even that wasn't enough sometimes. He fretted now and again how they would turn out.

He swiveled his attention to Rose. "What did your sister say to you about that meeting?"

The young woman glared at him, refusing to speak, but a sharp word from her granny unhinged her jaw.

"Honeysuckle recognized Pete," Rose growled. "She ain't—*wasn't* able to leave things alone. She went over to him an' called him out on who he was an' he 'fessed up. Said he was nervous because he didn't want nobody findin' out who he was."

Bass nodded. He had a writ on Pete Welker too.

"Honeysuckle wanted to send a message to her baby's daddy. Let him know he had a son." Rose's eyes gleamed wetly, but she didn't let any tears fall. She sipped a breath. "She had this damn fool idea that man would come runnin' back to her once he knew."

"Did he?"

"I never seen him." Rose clenched her jaw. "If I had, I'd have put a bullet between his eyes an' dropped him in a hole. He was nothin'. Just a man bringin' trouble. I knowed that the first time I seen him. Honeysuckle just never seen past them blue eyes."

Bass shifted his hat in his hands and felt uncomfortable. No matter how long he'd been in the peacekeeping business, talking about people's dead never got any easier. "I apologize for asking, but I need to know what happened to Honeysuckle."

For a moment, silence as cold and brittle as the first frost on a creek filled the cabin. Bass held up speaking further, not wanting to be the first to break the stillness. It was their story to tell, their grief to embrace and conquer.

Lucisa pulled a shawl from the back of her chair and pulled it across her shoulders. She shivered a little. She started to speak, then shook her head and looked at her granddaughter.

Mechanically, her face pale and tight, Rose looked past Bass, distancing herself from whatever she was remembering. "Just before daybreak, I went out early to do the milkin'. Like I been doin'. Before Honeysuckle had Nate, she'd go out with me, but since she had the baby, I tended to it myself. Let her sleep late as she could 'cause Nate—he could be a handful."

"That was thoughtful," Bass said. He tried to be easy, feeling his way around the hurt that threatened to burst the people before him.

"Honeysuckle took care of things when I got sick." Rose shrugged. "We looked out for one another. It's what sisters do."

Bass sat quiet and waited, knowing the young woman had to get to the rest of it in her own time.

"That mornin' I milked the cows an' come on back to the house. I noticed Honeysuckle wasn't up, an' neither was Nate." Her jaw quivered a little. "Wasn't like either of 'em. Usually, I got back, both of 'em was up an' about. I went back to their room, me an' Honeysuckle added a room on back before Nate was born, an' I found her there, but not Nate. He was gone. Honeysuckle—she was dead. Blood was ever'where."

Bass stood in the low doorway to the extra room; bending over some so he fit through it, but it didn't do any good because the door ran flush with the low ceiling. Scarcely eight feet square, hardly big enough for the bed and a small trunk of clothes, the room held a lot of emptiness now.

"I figure whoever killed her come through the window." Rose stood just back of Bass and peered around him. She still carried the rifle, but she made no effort to enter the room. Her hard eyes locked on the shuttered window. "The shutters are there to keep critters out. A man, though, he wouldn't—*didn't* have no trouble lifting the latch an' comin' on in. Then he killed Honeysuckle an' took Nate."

Bass swept the room with his gaze, but he knew he wasn't going to find anything. "Y'all cleaned the room?"

"I did. I didn't want Granny to have to do that, an' we couldn't leave it like it was." Rose ran a sleeve across her cheeks. "Granny could have done the cleanin'. She's buried my grandpa, my ma, an' my pa. Two of my brothers."

"Your granny has a lot of grit in her," Bass said.

"She stands tall when things got to be done."

"Did you find anything when you cleaned the room?"

"Nothin' that wasn't Honeysuckle's. Or Nate's."

"Okay then." Bass turned back to Rose. "You were planning on going after Pete Welker."

She fixed him with a hard stare. "I still am."

"No you're not," Lucisa called from the living room. "I lost your sister, girl. An' that little angel. I ain't gonna lose you too."

Bass waited.

"You hear me, Rose?"

The young woman swore silently but Bass could read her lips just fine. "Yes, Granny."

"Then you go ahead on an' tell the marshal about Paul's Valley."

That caught Bass's attention. He knew Paul's Valley because he'd been through there several times on business. The town lay over eighty miles west of Stringtown and was a major crossroads through the Chickasaw Nation.

Rose narrowed her eyes and spoke through clenched teeth. "Honeysuckle told me Nate's father lived in Paul's Valley."

"Why didn't she go there?" Bass asked.

"She was plannin' to before she was...before she couldn't."

"Your sister waited this long to plan that trip?"

"Honeysuckle didn't find out where he was till Pete told her in town. He was drunk an' talked too much. Rumor was Muskrat's gang ran on down to Texas, maybe clean to Mexico in order to escape the law. Pete said they was holed up in Paul's Valley now. Doin' business of some kind."

"That's a long trip."

"Mister, I'd have done been there if I coulda found someone to look after Granny an' got her to let me go. If you think it's a long trip, maybe you could stick around, watch over Granny, an' I'll ride on over there."

"Ma'am, I respect your dedication, but that ain't for you to do."

Anger tinted Rose's cheeks pink. Her free hand balled into a fist. "It's somethin' needs doin'."

Bass nodded. "And I'll see it gets done."

On the second night after he left the Paul house in the holler, Bass sat with his back to an oak tree and gazed up at the star-filled sky a short distance from the banked campfire. He was close enough that some of the heat soaked into him, dulling the night's chill, but not so close that the low light plucked him out of the shadows. The smell of smoke and cooked meat hung in the air. His rifle lay alongside his right leg.

They'd camped in a small clearing atop a hill that gave Bass a good vantage point for seeing anyone that might try to slip up on them.

Alfred slept near the horses, bundled up in a blanket that blended in with the surrounding ground. The old Indian was awake, though. His hand had curled around the rifle under the blanket.

When they were on the road, they traveled with a chuck wagon and a cook. This time out, Bass had hired Woody Hill to handle the meals and the wagon. Blooded in the Civil War, the old man slept under the chuck wagon. He snored almost loud enough to shake the timbers.

Bass and Alfred took turns keeping watch. Even off the trail as they were, they took care to be watchful. Troubles cropped up because others rode off the trails too, and most of those wanderers did so in an effort to avoid lawful folks.

The crickets quieted over to Bass's left and the grass rustled, giving physical presence to the uncomfortable feeling that tracked across the back of his neck like a trail of ants. He kept watching the stars, thinking about all he had still yet to do, and wondering if he was going to find Piebald and Muskrat and the little boy.

"Ain't no sense in you just sitting out there, Miss Paul," Bass said a few minutes later. "It's warmer here by the fire. And if you want, there's a bite of stew still left in the pot by the fire. I told Woody to put on extra because I knew you'd likely be catching up with us tonight."

The night chirping, clicks, and whistles continued in the woods around him. Except over in that dark patch to his left.

"That's all the invitation I got for you, Miss Paul," Bass said. "You can stay out there and be cold if you want, but I reckon you rode that horse hard today to catch up with us. Likely, you and that animal both need a night's rest." He folded his arms over his broad chest and waited.

Several minutes dragged by.

Finally, a shadow stood up to his left. The firelight flickered over Rose Paul as she stood there in her man's clothing and a flat-brimmed hat that looked beat-up and too big for her.

"You knew it was me?" she asked.

"Yep. Me and Alfred saw you cutting our trail just after noon. Knew you was following us."

She stood there for a minute, thinking. Bass knew it was probably hard to put her thoughts together because she was fatigued and he wasn't acting like she'd figured.

"You ain't gonna try to get me to go home?" she asked.

"Would you if I told you to?"

"No."

"Ain't no sense in me telling you that, then, is it?"

"Reckon not."

"Your granny taken care of?"

"She is. I got a neighbor's girl to stay with her 'til I get back."

"Trust that girl?"

"Martha's done it before. Gives her a rest from takin' care of all her brothers and sisters."

"I suppose that works out for all of you."

"Granny's gonna be mad all the same."

Bass grinned. "Sure glad she's not gonna be mad at me."

Rose cursed, then shifted in the grass. "I'm gonna go get my horse."

"You do that, Miss Paul, and make sure you get her squared away before you take care of yourself."

"I ain't no tenderfoot, Marshal. I know how to take care of a horse."

"Just making sure, because you sure ain't much for listening to folks."

Before first light the next morning, Bass stood looking down at Rose Paul sleeping twisted up in a thin blanket, her head on her saddle. Her boots stood at one end of the saddle.

The girl looked even younger in sleep, almost childlike. Dirt smeared her cheeks and sticks and grass littered her hair. During the night, she'd whimpered now and again, plaintive cries of hurt and loss.

"She's going to be trouble." Alfred stood at Bass's side. "I want to go into this telling you that."

Bass handed the posseman one of the tin cups of coffee he had poured at the chuck wagon. Woody Hill always put on chicory coffee and made it better than any cook Bass had ever had.

"So you can remind me later how you told me that?"

Alfred held the cup in both hands, letting the warmth soak into his fingers. "Yep."

"I figure she'll be less trouble riding with us than following. We can keep an eye on her here."

Alfred snorted, turned, and walked away.

Hating to do it because Rose was sleeping good now, Bass lightly kicked her foot.

Whirling under the covers like a startled bobcat, Rose hauled up her rifle and swung it around.

With his free hand, Bass caught the weapon by the barrel and held it away from him and the camp so it would fire harmlessly into the woods if she pulled the trigger. Fear widened the woman's eyes, then she realized where she was and she tried to cover the reaction.

Bass felt bad about scaring her, a little, but he reckoned it was a good reminder of how out of her depth she currently was. He needed her a little bit scared, enough to be cautious. But not enough to do something stupid. It was a fine balance.

"You awake now?" Bass asked.

"Yeah. Let go of my rifle."

"Wanted to make sure you didn't shoot anybody."

Rose grimaced and tugged to free the weapon.

Bass released the rifle. "Time to get up if you're gonna pull out with us this morning."

"I'm gettin' up." Using the rifle as a support, Rose heaved herself to her feet with no effort. He envied her the easy way she moved. Young bones took the hard ground better than his.

"Breakfast is ready," Woody called from the chuck wagon. "Come an' get it."

Rose pulled her boots on, adjusted her clothing, clapped her hat on her head, and started toward the wagon.

"Feed and water your horse first," Bass said.

She snarled a curse just loud enough for him to hear, then stomped toward the picket line where the horses stood.

Alfred laughed. "Yep. I can see how keeping an eye on her is going to be so much better."

Bass frowned at his posseman, but Alfred turned away and ignored him.

When they reached the outskirts of Paul's Valley three days later, Rose's eyes got big and she looked unsettled. The town sat at the bottom of a cluster of low hills on the other side of the meandering Washita River. The tributary curled and whipped like a broke-back snake before disappearing to the north and the south in the scrub woods. The streets were more or less straight and lined with clapboard buildings containing shops, restaurants, and hotels. Paul's Valley was a small town, but it was growing as the railroad came in.

"You feeling okay, Miss Paul?" Bass asked.

Rose pursed her lips and narrowed her eyes at him in a rebuff that Bass had seen before on the faces of his daughters, and sometimes his missus.

"I'm fine," Rose replied. "I just ain't never seen no town this big. Took me a minute to take it all in, is all."

"Why this here ain't nothin'," Woody Hill called from the chuck wagon's seat as he drove his mule team along the dusty road leading to Paul's Valley. "You want to see somethin' big, you should go take a look at Fort Smith or Saint Louie. But N'Orleans has got 'em all beat. That town's something to see. An' when the sun goes down? Why that's when the party really gets started. Got dead folks like to join the livin' ones."

Rose shook her head. "Ain't interested in big towns. I finish my business here, I'm gonna go back to the holler."

"While we're in town," Bass said, "I'll expect you to be mindful of what I say, Miss Paul. Follow where I lead and do as I say do. I intend to get you back to your granny alive."

"An' if I ain't wishful of listenin' to you?" Rose glared a challenge at him.

"Then I'll lock you in a cell for your own safety and my peace of mind until I get your nephew back."

She glared at him in disbelief. "You wouldn't."

"I would. If I was you, I'd keep in mind that I'm giving you the benefit of the doubt at the moment. On account of me being generous." Bass also wasn't sure the local peacekeepers could manage the young woman. He'd rather keep her where he could see her.

She got stiff-backed, but she didn't say another word all the way into town.

"I've seen the man you're describing, Marshal." Chickasaw Lighthorseman Holden Thorpe sat behind the desk in the small jailhouse that housed the tribal police. Young and lean, short-cropped black hair and dark eyes that advertised his Indian blood, he dressed neat in an ironed shirt and new jeans. He spoke in a quiet, cultured voice. "That man has been around town for the last few months. He says his name is Patrick McGee, but most people call him Pat."

"Pat's not a far cry from Pete." Bass sat on the other side of the old desk with a fresh cup of coffee in hand. "Name like that would make it easy to answer both ways, so a man wouldn't make a mistake hiding out."

"I was already thinking that."

From the way Holden's eyes took in Bass and his companions when they'd first met, the young Lighthorseman didn't miss much.

"Where have you seen him?" Bass asked.

"Usually, about this time, he's at the Badger, one of the local general stores, spending his time with the wrong people."

"'The wrong people?'"

A small smile lit Holden's face. "When you do this business in the same town long enough, Marshal, you learn who the *wrong* people are."

"You been here long enough?"

"I grew up here. These people are my people. This town is a good town,

*"Then I'll lock you in a cell for your own safety and my peace of mind."*

despite growing so much. Railroads have a tendency to do that to towns. I work to keep things peaceable. Which I'm so interested in the man you call Piebald."

Alfred sat outside keeping watch over the street. Rose occupied herself gazing at the stack of wanted flyers on a bookshelf across from the potbellied stove that kept the coffee pot and the room warm. From the speed the young woman shuffled through the flyers, just looking at the images, Bass suspicioned that she couldn't read any better than he could. She was just checking faces. And, occasionally, she was watching Holden Thorpe.

"Who are these *wrong* people Pat McGee's keeping time with?" Bass asked.

"It's an ongoing investigation."

"And you don't care to have it mucked up."

"Nope."

"That's a fine shirt you're wearing."

Holden's eyes narrowed and a glint of hostility showed. "You want to clarify that statement, Marshal?" His tone remained conversational, but his words carried an edged warning now. "In case I get the wrong idea?"

"You ever notice how clothing's made? How everything fits together? Until you get one loose thread?" Bass held up a finger. "Just one. That's all it takes. You get one loose thread, you pull on it, that whole shirt might come apart."

"We're not talking about my shirt, are we?"

Bass smiled. "Nope. We're talking about Piebald. He's that one loose thread we got to work with. Either you and I can pull it together, or I'll tug on it my ownself. I got paper on him and you don't. Right now I'm giving you a choice." He paused, took Holden's measure and saw the Lighthorseman wasn't just going to roll over. "I'm looking at Piebald for the murder of a young woman and the kidnapping of her child. What can you ante up?"

"Piebald has been keeping company with men that's suspected of horse thievery outside of town."

"No witnesses?"

"None left alive. A month ago, Reid Taylor and his brother got shot and killed during the theft of their horses. I've been keeping an eye on the men I think did that when I can. Piebald has been riding with them of late."

"Then these are all bad men. We want them to pay for whatever crimes they've been doing."

"We do." Holden stood. "Let me get my hat and let Lonnie, the jailer, know I'm walking you down to the Badger."

The Badger Mercantile stood two stories tall and featured a stuffed brown full-grown badger that hung from a sign over the batwing doors. Someone had climbed up and hung from the eaves to stuff a cigar in the badger's mouth and put a child-size bowler hat on it. Rain and moths had been at the badger, though, and it didn't look like it was going to hang there much longer before it came apart at the seams.

"I hope you don't mind me saying so, Miss Paul," Holden said as he led the way across the rutted dirt street between wagons and horsemen, "but this place isn't a proper venue for a young woman."

"You look out for yourself," Rose told him. "A town boy like you don't look like you'd make the cut in the holler where I come from. I can take care of myself just fine."

Holden winced and looked at Bass for support. Bass kept a smile from his face, but only because he knew they were headed into potential trouble.

Rose and Holden reached the batwing doors at the same time, and each of them pushed on through the door in front of them. Bass stepped through the open doors after them, slitting his eyes to adjust to the dim afternoon lighting streaking the general store. He removed his hat since he was indoors.

Quiet fell over the interior, maybe because the regulars recognized Holden, or maybe because they recognized Rose wasn't exactly the kind of woman they were used to seeing there. A couple of sales girls working the small crowd gathered around the dining tables shot Rose mean-tempered glares as their prospective clients got interested in something they hadn't had before.

A group of six men in cowboy dress occupied a large table in the other corner of the room. To a man, they were all rough trade, unwashed for the most part, whites and Indians alike. They watched Holden and Bass with hard eyes, but they also watched Rose with an entirely different intent. Bass hoped the young woman didn't notice. If she did, she gave no indication.

Racks and shelves held dry goods and folded clothing. Boots and moccasins occupied built-in shelving that shared space with saddles and leather goods. Bass noted most of the inventory held a layer of dust. The Badger might claim to be a general store, but the front of the house sales and the small kitchen weren't paying the bills.

Walking to the back of the mercantile, Holden sat at a square table surrounded by mismatched chairs. Bass leaned his rifle against the wall. Rose stood hers beside her chair where it would be quick to hand.

The store clerk, a heavy-set Indian man with a prominent broken nose, glanced over at Holden. "Coffee?"

Holden nodded.

"You got sandwiches?" Bass asked. He smelled baked bread and his stomach rumbled.

"I do. Got ham and onion, fried chicken baskets, taters—mashed and baked, and fresh baked bread."

Bass looked at Rose. "You hungry?"

"No."

"My treat." Bass suspected she had lit out with not much money, if any at all.

"I'm fine. Had a big breakfast."

"I'm not gonna say nothing against Woody's cooking, but breakfast was hours ago." Bass shifted his attention back to the clerk. "Give me a whole chicken, mashed taters, and two of them ham and onion sandwiches."

The clerk smiled. "Coming up. Coffee?"

Bass nodded and smiled. He'd learned it was easier to buy something and earn good graces from folks. Holden, being local, didn't have to do that.

One of the sales clerks brought over a coffee pot and three ceramic cups. She put sugar and cream on the table as well.

"Thank you, ma'am," Bass said.

After she left, Holden spoke in a low voice that didn't carry. "Once upon a time, the Badger was a decent place for folks, when it was operated by George Buckram, the present owner's grandfather. George Buckram and his wife were good friends with Smith Paul, the man who founded the town."

The young peace officer's voice held a wistful note Bass couldn't miss. "Times change."

Holden nodded. "They do. The last two generations of Buckrams have maintained this place, but it's turned into an outlaw hangout. Used to be, men gathered here to trade goods and services. Now you get lowlifes like those men over there," he flicked his eyes to the rough trade crowd in the corner, "looking to hook up with other men dealing in illicit goods and services."

"Is that a fact?"

"There's rumors of gun running, horse thieving, and whiskey smuggling. More stories about young women who have been taken down to Mexico and sold." Holden cut his eyes to Rose. "Pardon my frankness, Miss Paul."

"It's nothin' I ain't heard about before," Rose replied. "You grow up a female in the Territories, you hear them stories. It's something else you look out for. Like timber rattlers an' water moccasins an' feral hogs."

"I'm sure that's true." In spite of her assurances, Holden didn't look comfortable. He rubbed his shaven jaw with a callused hand.

"If you know those are bad men, why haven't you arrested them?" Bass asked.

"Because I'd have to be able to prove those charges in a court of law, Marshal."

"Ain't nobody pressed charges?"

"No one who's pressed charges has lived long enough to go to court. After the first three people ended up with their tongues cut out, and after the Taylor brothers were gunned down at their place during the horse theft, no one wants to speak out against them." A grim look settled over Holden's face, and it made him appear older. "They're careful, and that makes them hard and dangerous to catch."

The saleswoman delivered the chicken basket, mashed potatoes, and sandwiches. Ruby hesitated only a moment, but after Bass nodded to her, she tucked in with gusto.

While he ate, Bass thought about the situation. "How long has it been since the last horse theft?"

"Almost six weeks," Holden answered.

"How far apart do they usually hit?"

"Usually no more than a month."

"So they're overdue."

"Horse theft isn't exactly the weather," Holden said.

Bass smiled. "Maybe not, but it's been my experience that most career criminals tend to run out of money regular. Makes a lot of them desperate, and desperate is its own timetable. I suppose all the horse ranches around town have posted extra guards."

"They have."

"That ain't gonna stop them."

Holden blew out a breath. "I know." His eyes narrowed as he gazed through the mercantile's windows. "You know that loose thread you were talking about?"

"Yeah." Bass cut his gaze to the front of the store and spotted Piebald getting down off his horse.

Pete "Piebald" Welker wrapped his reins around the hitching post in front of the mercantile. Another rider, this one dressed in a suit and wearing a broad-brimmed Stetson, dismounted, called out, and tossed his reins to Piebald, who wrapped them around the hitching post as well.

Together, the two men entered the Badger with their spurs ringing.

Beside Bass, Rose started to get to her feet. Evidently she'd had no problem recognizing Piebald as well.

Bass dropped a big hand on the young woman's arm, wrapping his fingers around her forearm and the chair arm. "Stay sit," he ordered in a hoarse whisper.

She glared at him and tried to yank her arm free, but it didn't budge. "That's him!" she whispered back.

Bass returned her hot gaze full measure and willed her stubbornness to go away. "I know who that is, and if you want that baby boy back, you leave this be and let me handle things. Do you understand?"

Rose whispered some sharp words, some that probably surprised Holden regarding her knowledge of such matters, but she nodded and turned her attention back to the chicken basket. She could even chew angry.

Piebald and his companion showed no hesitation about joining the rough trade group. The men scooted around the table to make room for Piebald and the other man as they brought chairs over from another table.

"Who's the dandy?" Bass asked.

"That," Holden replied, "is Nathan Clifford. Have you heard of him?"

"Name rings a bell."

It wasn't a big leap to figure Honeysuckle Paul had named her baby after his father. From Rose's sudden intake of breath, Bass suspicioned the young woman had put two and two together as well.

"His father is Edward Clifford."

That name whistled like a circus calliope. Bass watched the young man with renewed interest. "Edward Clifford is a big to-do in these parts."

"He is. Clifford owns property here and over in Tishomingo, and a ranch down in Gainesville, Texas. For the time being, he's living in Paul's Valley, setting up new business dealings with the railroad people. People say he's going to make himself another fortune at that."

"I've heard he's a smart man."

"He is."

"So what's his boy doing spending time with the riffraff?"

"Nathan Clifford isn't as smart as his father, but he's just as greedy." Holden eyed the man across the room. "My thinking is that with his father nailing down all honest and mostly honest business around here, Nathan's cutting what he can from illegal profits."

"You can't prove that."

"No, but I'd like to. Nathan's learned enough from his father to cover his tracks, and they know all the tribal policemen in the area. I had a criminal go in undercover, but I haven't seen him since. I don't know if he just ran off or if he's been buried out in the woods somewhere."

Bass smiled. "Maybe now that we got that one thread we been talking about..."

Three days later, at night, Bass sat at the table with the rough trade at the Badger like he had the last two nights. He was dressed like a cowboy in faded clothes, rundown boots, and Mexican-made chaps that had seen better days. He wore a floppy gray sombrero with years old mud stains and crossed ammunition belts loaded with cartridges for the Buffalo Sharps .50-caliber rifle canted up against the wall behind him.

Even though the men had all seen him in Holden Thorpe's company three days ago, none of them recognized him as the same man. Long ago, he'd learned to be a chameleon among such men, and they would swear that he was shorter than he was because he'd learned to disguise his height too by holding himself differently.

As "Pedro Martinez," cow thief and ex-bullfighter, Bass was a talker, a schemer, and a man who claimed to have done any number of things. At the moment, he regaled them with stories of the bulls he'd fought in Barcelona, Spain, and of the pretty senoritas that had claimed his favors. He knew of such things from men he'd met, and from bullfights he'd seen down in Mexico when he'd traveled across the border.

"This bull, Murciélago, which is Spanish for 'bat,' must have been part bat," Bass said in a quiet voice designed to draw in his listeners. "No matter which way I went, that killer come for me again and again. Them horns missed by inches, chopped my shirt and pants to shreds, and I was bleeding from a half-dozen cuts. I couldn't get away from him."

"Maybe he could smell you," Merle Turlock said. He was a whiskey runner Bass had paper on, and the description matched the man down to the two missing fingers on his left hand and the mangled remains of his left ear, which had reportedly been gnawed on by a grizzly.

Bass shook his head. "Bulls can't smell that good. They ain't like horses. Nope, this one, I think he was listenin' to my heart beatin' inside my chest. An' I knowed he could, because it sounded like an axe striking hardwood. I could hear it my ownself, an' I thought it was gonna jump right outta my chest."

"Then what happened?" Milton Moss asked. He was the youngest one of the men clustered around the table and didn't have any paper on him that Bass knew of. But he'd fallen in with the other cutthroats and his hands were likely as bloody as anyone's there.

"Why, he put me up against the wall, locked me in between his horns. I grabbed onto him so he couldn't back away an' gore me before I could get away." Bass held his curled hands out to his sides like he was holding the bull's horns.

Milton shook his head. "What happened?"

"I knowed I was holdin' my own life in my hands, along with them horns," Bass said. "So when the bull pulled away, I couldn't let go. He dragged me after him, then stopped an' got ready to charge me again. I took that one minute, that thin minute, an' I set my boots as good as I could. I set 'em deep. Then when ol' Murciélago started to charge again, why I whipped them horns around hard as I could because I knowed I only had the one chance. His neck snapped like a rifle shot. Plumb sickenin' is what it was. Then he dropped there at my feet, dead as a doornail."

Milt slapped Bass on the shoulder. "Whooeee! Wished I coulda seen that! I ain't never seen nobody snap a bull's neck before!"

In the corner, Candy Tucker shook his head and made a sour face. The man was large and beefy and wore a Bowie knife strapped to his left hip in a cross draw rig. His long, greasy hair brushed his broad shoulders. When he breathed out, his breath stank of whiskey. "How is it you're believin' any of this, Milt?"

Blinking in confusion, Milt drew back and looked like his feelings had been hurt. "What do you mean, Candy?"

"I mean," Candy said, leaning forward, "that Pedro is fulla hot air, an' these stories of his ain't nothin' but stories."

"Why would he lie?" Milt asked.

Candy cursed. "Because fools like you an' some of the others at this table listen to him, of course." He glared at Bass. "That's why."

Bass had been expecting trouble from Candy. The man liked to be the center of attention, and probably had been until the last couple of days. Bass had deliberately set out to steal his thunder.

Turning in his chair to his left, Bass addressed the man. "I don't hold with no man callin' me a liar."

"Well, you're gonna hold with it tonight, Pedro."

"No sir, I ain't."

"You don't wanna poke the bear, amigo." Candy's right hand dropped down to the Bowie's hilt. "An' if you try to reach for that rifle, I'll gut you. In fact, you're gonna get up right now an' leave it behind, an' you ain't gonna come back here no more."

The men around the table backed off.

"I'll tell you one thing for certain," Bass said in an easy tone, "I ain't leavin' that rifle. Been over the mountain with it, an' it goes with me."

Candy pulled the Bowie in a practiced flicker that showed years of experience and practice. The ten-inch blade gleamed in the lantern light as it streaked for Bass's throat.

Ducking back, Bass caught Candy's wrist in his right hand and stopped the cruelly curved point only inches from his Adam's apple. At the same time, he thrust his left forearm against his attacker's elbow, got his weight behind it, and shattered the joint.

The Bowie dropped from Candy's fingers as the man squalled in pain. Then, breathing hard, he shouted, "Kill him, Darrell!"

Across the table, Darrell Tucker, a smaller, younger version of his brother, stood and reached for his pistol. By the time Darrell had his weapon out, Bass released Candy's arm and reached for Darrell's pistol. Before Darrell could ear the pistol's hammer back, Bass closed his fist around his opponent's weapon and hand, set himself, and yanked the man across the table.

Whirling, levering the man over his hip, Bass whipped Darrell to the floor. Still holding onto the captured weapon and hand, Bass slammed a boot heel right between Darrell's eyes. The man's eyes rolled white and he fell back limp.

Breathing only a little harder, Bass took Darrell's pistol and looked back at the crowd at the table. "Anybody else don't like my stories?"

"Nope," Merle Turlock said in a quiet voice. "Me an' the rest of the boys, we like your stories. Like 'em just fine."

In the small hours before morning, Bass woke in the grungy hotel room he'd rented in Pedro Martinez's name. He wore pants and his shirt, but he answered the door in his stockinged feet and a pistol in hand.

Three men stood out in the hallway and he knew them all. Piebald and Nathan Clifford looked pretty much the same as they had when he'd seen them. But it was his first time to lay eyes on Elton "Muskrat" Mater. The man looked hard and mean, balding and bearded, and as cold-eyed as a Louisiana gator.

Bass's stomach tensed and he wondered how this was going to play out. He knew manhandling the Tucker brothers was going to force something, but he had no way of knowing what that would be.

Alfred was nearby and Rose Paul was with Woody Hill, safe in another hotel, much to her irritation and vocal dissatisfaction. Getting out of the room quicklike was gonna be hard to do, though.

If it went that way.

"Can I help you?" Bass held the door open on a few inches. So far nobody but him had a gun in his hand.

Nathan Clifford smiled. "Senor Pedro Martinez."

"That's me." Bass eased back the .44's hammer but kept showing a confused smile.

"My name is Nathan Clifford. The Tucker brothers work for me."

"Listen. If this is about that dust-up at the Badger, them boys…"

Nathan Clifford held up a hand and nodded. "Candy has got a big mouth. You work with the man, you learn that. And his brother will do anything he tells him to do. I know they started the fracas, and you finished it a lot faster than anybody thought you would."

"Things like that tend to happen fast."

"I was impressed when Mr. McGee told me about it."

Piebald nodded.

"I was even more impressed when you didn't want the police called in."

"I ain't got much use for police, tell you the truth. An' I don't want none of them lookin' too hard at me, if you know what I mean."

"I think I do. However, Candy isn't going to be able to work for a while, what with that broken arm, and his brother is throwing up and can't walk straight. The doc thinks he's got a concussion."

"They come at me pretty sudden, Mr. Clifford. If I coulda been more gentle…"

"That's their own lookout," Nathan Clifford said. "However, I find myself short of hands for my latest project."

"I apologize. Didn't mean to cause nobody no hardship." Bass waited, hoping things would go the way he wanted.

"And I accept. However, I thought I might extend a business proposition to you. Given what you've told Mr. McGee and his cohorts, you don't mind breaking a few laws."

"I'm listenin'."

"I've got some horses outside of town that I need to move down to Texas."

Anger flickered through Bass but he kept it under control. His plan might have gotten him in with the gang, but it hadn't stopped the horse thievery. He wondered if the latest victims were still alive, knowing he'd feel bad if they weren't.

"Are you any good at moving horses, Mr. Martinez?" Nathan Clifford asked.

With effort, Bass smiled. "As it turns out, Mr. Clifford, I am."

"Good. We'll discuss wages along the trail, but I'm sure we'll find a number we agree on."

"Yes sir. Thank you for the opportunity."

"You're welcome, but you made this opportunity yourself."

"Didn't know I was gonna do that. Purely glad it worked out this way, though."

"You're happier about it than the Tucker brothers," Muskrat said. His grin deepened, but remained pure evil. "I guess they need to be happy they're still alive."

"I don't know about the younger brother, but Candy had him a skin full." Bass shook his head. "God looks out for drunkards most times. I try to look out for 'em too."

Nathan Clifford frowned at that. "I'd heard about Mr. Tucker's inebriation. After I deal with this bit of business, I'll be talking to him about that." He smiled again. "In the meantime, I need to know if you'll be ready to pull out tomorrow morning. I've got an appointment set up, and I don't want to be late for it. My father taught me that punctuality is important in business."

"Yes sir. I'll be ready. You just tell me where."

"One other thing." Clifford reached under his jacket. For a moment, Bass tensed up and dropped his finger over the trigger of his pistol. Then his gut unclenched when the man produced a cigar. "Have a smoke. I'm celebrating. I'm a father." He grinned widely.

Bass accepted the cigar. "Well, congratulations then."

The next afternoon, Bass rode drag on a string of stolen horses and celebrated his newfound fame with the owlhoots who worked for Nathan Clifford and Muskrat. He kept a bandana over his nose and mouth and tried to blink away all the grit from his eyes that floated in the dust clouds raised by the horses.

Fatigue hung over Bass because he hadn't slept much. After Nathan Clifford's visit, he signaled to Alfred in a hotel across the street. The old man had climbed up the side of the building in the shadows without being seen and conferred with Bass.

The plan was for Bass to ride with Muskrat's gang and find out what Nathan Clifford's "business" was before they figured out what they were going to do with the outlaws. If everything had gone as Bass had wished, Alfred wouldn't alert Holden Thorpe about the operation till after the horses were nearly to Texas. Bass wanted to see the other end of the arrangement as well.

When a nest of rattlers got stirred up, sometimes it was hard to keep track of which way they were going. If a man wasn't careful, he'd get bit.

They made the eighty-mile trip down to Gainesville, crossing the Red River along the way, in four days without seeing another soul. It was good time, seeing as how they were moving forty-three head of horses that sometimes didn't want to go in the direction they were supposed to go. But it was still a hard time in the saddle, riding all day and sleeping under the stars. Every day reminded Bass he wasn't as young as he'd been.

The meeting took place in a small clearing under spreading oak trees covered in spring's fresh leaves. The sight made Bass think about the illustration he'd seen in Frank Leslie's Illustrated Newspaper. In that picture, men with hangmen's nooses around their necks lined tree branches.

It had been called the Great Hanging at Gainesville, and all told, forty-one Unionists had gotten strung up by the Citizens Court. It was a sorrowful thing to do because the men hadn't taken part in the fighting. They'd just disapproved of secession.

And maybe some of the men who'd voted to hang them had been after their land. Or maybe it had just been men's desires to kill other men. That one never seemed to grow old.

After they'd been in the clearing for a few hours, another group arrived

*"My father taught me that punctuality is important in business."*

in wagons. It didn't take Bass long to put together the horse trading was for whiskey, which was illegal in the Territories. Nathan Clifford, according to Milt, had folks in the Territories that bought wholesale and sold the liquor to individuals.

Since the horses were stolen on Indian land, most likely from Chickasaw and Choctaw ranchers, Nathan Clifford didn't have any money invested in his business and none of the owners would ride down to Texas because they couldn't leave the Territories.

The arrangement was all profit. Horseflesh translated into whiskey and multiplied the take.

Bass didn't have any jurisdiction in Texas, but he memorized faces of the other men involved in case they ever showed up north of the Red River. They were all hard men, a crew like Muskrat's, and he was certain they'd put in an appearance there if they got cash hungry or in trouble in Texas.

Within the hour, Nathan Clifford had completed his business and they were back on the trail into the Territories. Muskrat and his men got to "sample" some of the whiskey along the way and became a rowdy bunch.

The following night Nathan Clifford halted the caravan on the south side of the Red River, intending to take up the ride again in the morning. Bass played into his Pedro persona, telling stories, all of them whoppers that young Milt hung onto, with humor that made the other outlaws roll. He'd played Pedro several times before and enjoyed the role.

Afterwards, he volunteered for first watch and set up on the outer perimeter, regretting the distance he sat from the campfires. For an hour or two, he sat with his back to a tree and listened to the men grow quiet and still, watched the firelight settle down to a steady glow, and tried to relax. An owl called somewhere in the distance.

"Seems like your new friends really like you."

Alfred's warm breath in Bass's ear startled him. He barely kept himself from heaving himself to his feet. Waiting a beat, he took a deep breath and let it out.

"Stop sneaking up on me," Bass whispered.

"I didn't sneak. I did the owl call. Like we agreed."

"I thought we agreed you'd do a mockingbird."

Alfred shook his head. "You never listen."

"You never remember." Bass waved that away. "I take it you didn't have any trouble trailing my horse."

"I wouldn't even have needed the notched horseshoe. Not many people running horses down this way. Ground was all tore up. Your Lighthorseman had trouble at times, comes from living in a town too much. But I kept him and the other tribal policemen squared away."

"You've got an ambush spot picked out?"

"We do. About a mile up from the river. We'll be tracking you as you cross. By the time you ford the river, the horses and the men will be tuckered out."

"That sounds good." Bass took a breath. "I'll be glad when this is over."

"We do have one problem, though."

Bass closed his eyes. "Rose."

"Yep. She noticed we pulled out of Paul's Valley and lit out after us. Holden Thorpe and I tried to talk sense into her, but she wasn't in the mood to listen."

"She didn't like getting cut out of things."

"Nope. Told you she would be trouble."

"So where is she now?"

"Around. Somewhere. I see her every now and again, but she's stayed away. She's good in the brush, and I've had my hands full with the tribal policemen."

"Keep Rose out of this," Bass said.

"Not my choice, but I'll do what I can."

Bass thanked Alfred and the old man disappeared without a sound. A minute later, an owl called out again. Bass didn't know if it was his posseman or the real thing.

Just before noon, as his horse gained dry ground on the north side of the Red River, Bass looked up at a familiar metallic clicking and saw Muskrat pointing a .44 at his face.

"You want to tell me what this is about?" Bass asked, feeling his mouth go dry. He couldn't figure out what had happened. All that morning everyone had acted the same.

"It ain't nothin' personal, Pedro," Muskrat said. "It's just I'm not a man who likes to take chances."

Atop his mount, Nathan Clifford looked on with a knotted face. "I'm sorry, Mr. Martinez, but I allow Mr. Mater to conduct business with the employees. He is a cautious man, and I pay him to do that. I didn't agree with him until this morning. He can be quite convincing when he sets his mind to it."

"Muskrat," Milt pleaded, "you don't have to do this. Pedro's a good man."

"A good man?" Muskrat spat into the tall grass, speaking loud enough to be heard over the rush of the river. "He comes around you people, a man ain't none of you ever seen before, and takes out two of our guys right before we have this trip set up. That don't make none of y'all suspicious?"

"It was just bad luck," Milt said. "Candy and Darrell, they's the ones that started the fracas. Wasn't Pedro."

"Yeah," Bass said. "Wasn't me."

Wind blew through Muskrat's hair, lifting it from his bald spot. "If it was just bad luck, I'm sorry. But I'm gonna kill you either way. We needed you to help move the horses, but these wagons are easy enough. I'll give you a minute to ask for peace with your maker."

Bass cast his thoughts wide but couldn't come up with anything better than heeling his mount aside and attempting to dive into the river. Even if he succeeded, he was certain Muskrat would have no problem picking him off. He couldn't hold his breath forever, and the river didn't move fast enough to carry him away in time.

Muskrat suddenly jerked to one side and blood flew from his left shoulder. Shocked, he wheeled around just as the *cra-ack* of a rifle shot drifted over the area.

"Take cover!" Muskrat yelled. He ducked low over his horse and rode toward the trees.

Stunned, not certain what had happened, Bass headed his mount along the river bed, taking advantage of the steep bank to provide cover. The horse's hooves sank in the mud and made sucking sounds as they pulled free. He rode in the direction of the shooter, hoping whoever had shot Muskrat would be a friend. He thought maybe Alfred had drifted forward to keep an eye on things.

"Over here!" one of the outlaws yelled. "It's a girl!"

Rifles and pistols spat lead and thunder, filling the air with the noise of the gunfire.

Bass cursed, knowing the only "girl" that would most likely be in the area was Rose Paul. Spotting a gentler rise ahead through the scrub brush and cattails lining the river, he urged his horse up it. Thick mud clods whirled from under the horse's feet as it galloped up the incline and gained level ground.

Someone had spotted him because bullets hammered the trees and branches around him. He stayed low over the saddle pommel as leaves and twigs rained down over him. He pulled the Sharps buffalo rifle from the scabbard and rolled the hammer back.

Halting the horse behind a thick stand of blackjack trees, Bass hauled the heavy rifle to his shoulder, took aim at one of Muskrat's outlaws riding hellbent for the high and uncut, led him a little, let out part of his breath, and dropped the hammer. The Sharps kicked into Bass's shoulder like a country fed mule, bruising the flesh and jarring the bone.

The .50-caliber round slammed into the outlaw and knocked him from his saddle. From the loose way he dropped and hit the ground, Bass knew the man wasn't going to get up again. He felt bad about killing people. He hadn't done it much, and had never become accustomed to it. If Rose Paul hadn't been out there somewhere, he might have tried to talk the men into giving themselves up.

Cursing the fact that "Pedro" favored the big single-shot rifle, Bass worked the lever, sent the spent shell spinning, trailing smoke, and plucked a fresh cartridge from the belts across his chest. He rammed the cartridge home and took aim again. Before he could get settled, a hail of bullets smashed into his cover.

"He's got that Sharps rifle!" one of the outlaws yelled. "He won't be able to reload fast enough to get us all!"

Three outlaws wheeled their horses toward Bass. Holding the reins in one hand, they fired their rifles on the gallop, racing through the clouds of smoke streaming out of the barrels.

Bass took aim again, placing the sights over the center rider, and squeezing the trigger. When the .50-caliber round split the man's chest, he toppled over the rear of the horse and the animal bolted sideways, interfering with the rider on the left.

Knowing he didn't have time to reload the rifle, Bass held onto it and urged his horse forward toward the rider on the right. The outlaw's eyes opened wide in surprise when he spotted Bass riding toward him. The horses collided, chest to chest, and staggered. While the outlaw fired a round that heated the air only an inch from Bass's left ear, the marshal swung the Sharps hard as he could.

The heavy barrel smacked into the outlaw's temple, knocking him cold on impact. As the man slid bonelessly from the panicked horse, Bass wheeled his horse around, released the reins, and transferred the Sharps to his left hand. He drew one of his .44s as the third rider rounded the blackjacks.

Standing up in the stirrups, the outlaw levered his rifle to chamber a new cartridge and took aim at Bass from less than twenty feet away. Bass held his ground and fired at the man's chest. The bullet slapped into the man's right shoulder and jarred him right before he shot. The round went into the air. Before he could work the lever again, Bass rolled back the pistol's hammer and put a bullet through the man's heart.

Bass kicked his horse into motion and headed in the direction he guessed that Rose Paul had been hiding. Four riders converged on a low hill and Bass guessed the young woman had dug in there. As he watched, one of the men dropped from the saddle, then a fusillade of bullets chewed into the ridge of the hill, scattering grass and earth.

Making himself stay calm as the outlaws closed in on Rose's position, Bass fired at the three remaining men, hoping to distract them. Instead, his horse suddenly went down, falling limp so quick that he knew the animal was already dead. Bass threw himself from the saddle, hoping the horse didn't roll over on him. If he wasn't killed or hurt bad, the possibility of getting trapped under the dead animal remained a threat.

He hit the ground hard, felt the wind go out of his lungs in a rush, and lost the Sharps and the .44 somewhere in the tall grass. Senses reeling, he flopped over onto his stomach and willed his breath back into his body. Bullets cut the grass over his head and blades floated down over him.

Wheezing, ignoring the black spots dancing in his vision, Bass pulled his other pistol and rolled the hammer back as he stuck his head up. He'd lost the sombrero too.

Thirty yards away, Rose broke cover and ran, cradling her rifle in both hands. One of the riders bore down on her, but she took aim with the rifle and caused the man to dodge to the side. When she didn't shoot, Bass realized her weapon was empty.

The outlaws figured that out too, because they rode at her fearlessly then. The first rider reached down and caught her by the arm, yanking her up and draping her across his saddle. Rose fought back, but only succeeded in losing her rifle. The outlaw clubbed her in the head with his pistol and she lay still.

Knowing his pistol didn't have the distance he needed; Bass glanced around for the Sharps and spotted it lying a few yards distant. He sprinted for the rifle and scooped it up as bullets thudded into the ground around him. He ducked and rolled, feeling the aches and pains again as he slammed into the ground.

He was getting too old for this, but he couldn't imagine living his life any other way. His skills made a living for his family, and he took pride in his work.

Sure and smooth despite the gunfire, Bass scooped up the Sharps, opened the action, and slid a cartridge into the chamber. He spun and brought the rifle up, knowing he was visible to his foes. He peered down the long barrel, held it steady, and took aim, leading the rider a little. He was grateful Rose lay draped over the saddle.

He squeezed the trigger, rode out the massive recoil, and watched the rider and Rose tumble from the horse. As he reloaded the Sharps, he searched for the second rider, but only spotted the man's horse in the distance. He didn't know where the rider was, but the blood on the saddle led him to believe it had been Muskrat.

Back at the wagons, the surviving outlaws had taken up positions and fired steadily, driving Bass to ground behind the low hill where Rose had been. His breath blew into the ground, and he knew things looked bad for the girl and him.

She'd saved his life. There wasn't a doubt in his mind about that. If not for her shooting Muskrat, he'd have been cooling in the sun about now.

He lay the Sharps aside and reloaded both of his pistols, getting as ready as he could for what was to come.

"Hey, Pedro."

Tracking the voice, Bass spotted Muskrat getting to his feet in the tall grass. He held Rose Paul in front of him like a shield. Conscious again, the young woman stared blankly at Bass, like maybe not all of her senses had yet returned.

"Put that rifle down, Pedro," Muskrat said, "or I'm going to blow this woman's head off."

Bass hesitated, thinking that the only reason Muskrat hadn't already shot Rose was because he wanted to keep her for a while and use her any way he wanted. If that was true, it might be better if Bass took his chances with the rifle.

"Hey Piebald," Muskrat called out.

"Yeah," Pete Welker shouted from behind Bass.

"You got a bead on Pedro?"

"I do."

"If he doesn't put that Sharps down, shoot him."

"I will."

Bass looked over his shoulder but didn't turn away from Muskrat. About eighty yards away, Piebald took aim over the driver's seat of one of the whiskey wagons. The man would have to be good to make a killing shot.

Or lucky. A man could never discount luck.

"You see how it is, Pedro." Muskrat's voice mocked him. "I know you could shoot me through this girl, but I'm betting you won't do that. Who knows? Maybe I'm wrong."

Muskrat wasn't wrong. Even if the young woman was going to die at Muskrat's hands, Bass knew he couldn't be the one to kill her.

"Do it!" Muskrat snarled. "Drop them…"

Rose rammed the back of her head into Muskrat's nose, causing the man to cry out and curse in pain as he stumbled back with blood gushing into his beard. Before Muskrat recovered, Rose pulled a knife from her boot top and slammed it into her would-be captor's throat. Muskrat's pistol discharged harmlessly into the air.

A rifle cracked and Rose stumbled to one side, then fell at the same time Bass realized he wasn't the one that had been shot.

A chill touched Bass's heart as he spun and took aim. Piebald ducked behind the driver's seat, but his legs remained visible through the wagon spokes. Bass squeezed the trigger and the .50-caliber round tore through Piebald's left knee, tearing the limb to pieces and knocking him down.

Abandoning his position, Bass ran for the spot where Rose had gone down, hoping the young woman wasn't dead. Bullets pelted the ground around him for a moment and whispered through brush, then a fresh wave of gunshots split the air.

A glance over his shoulder showed Bass that Alfred and five Lighthorsemen were riding into the fray. The outlaws, including Nathan Clifford, threw down their weapons at once.

When Bass reached Rose, she was in a small gully that afforded her some measure of protection as she pulled the pistol from Muskrat's dead hand. She pulled the hammer back and rolled over, bringing the weapon to bear on Bass. Blood stained her right side, soaking her shirt and jacket.

Bass stopped and spread his hands wide. "Don't shoot."

Relaxing, she turned the pistol away. "Why aren't they shooting?"

Kneeling beside her, Bass sat the Sharps down and pulled her shirt and jacket away to reveal the wound. The bullet had just kissed her flesh and hadn't hit anything vital.

Luck. The young woman had to be plumb full of it.

Bass stood in front of the massive door in front of the large house and banged his knuckles hard even though he knew Edward Clifford was aware there were visitors. Bass was also certain Clifford knew who his visitors were. For a moment he continued waiting, looking around at the manicured grounds and thinking about how many men it took to keep such a place looking as good as it did. The trees were freshly trimmed and the lawn and flowers were immaculate.

Beside him, Rose Paul stood quietly, which was something Bass didn't expect. Maybe the wound had taken something out of her, but she was on the mend. He had no doubts she'd be back to her old, cantankerous self in no time.

The door opened and a polite older man in a simple black suit stood there.

"May I help you?" the man asked.

"I'm United States Marshal Bass Reeves." Bass put all the authority and command in his voice that he could muster. "I'm here to see Mr. Clifford."

"Mr. Clifford is not receiving visitors at the moment, I'm afraid."

Bass held up the writ in his hand. He couldn't read it, but he knew what it said. "This here paper says I can see him. Now you can either let me in or I can walk right over you, but I'm coming through this door."

"It's all right, Evans," another man's voice said. "I'll take care of this."

Bass stepped into the house as the butler moved away. The marshal carried a rifle in his hand that wasn't holding the writ.

Edward Clifford came to a stop ten feet from the door. The man was an older version of his son, except he'd gone gray and weighed a little more. Still, that same sense of entitlement clung to him, strong as skunk scent.

"You can't just barge into my home," Clifford protested.

"This paper here, from Judge Parker's court, says I can do anything I want in these premises. Including arresting anyone who gets in my way. So we can do this easy or hard. You can choose it up."

Clifford took the paper from Bass and quickly read through the print. "It says here you've come for my grandson."

"No," Bass said, "I've come for Miss Paul's nephew."

"You can't just take him."

"Mr. Clifford, that baby is part Chickasaw Indian, and Judge Parker sits to take care of Indian affairs in these territories. As a member of the Chicksaws…"

"He's not a member of the Chickasaws. I'm his grandfather."

"…custody of a child goes through the mother's people. Matriarchal rights are observed."

Clifford turned his gaze to Rose. "Miss Paul?"

"I am," Rose said in a hard voice.

"I know about your family. I know that you people live rough. Don't you understand that I can provide that baby a better life than you can?"

"Mr. Clifford, with all due respect, even though I don't figure you deserve any an' I'm only sayin' it to be polite, not that you deserve that neither," Rose said, "I seen how boys turn out that you raise. Yours fathered a child and ran off when he found out he was gonna be a daddy. An' he was a horse thief an' a whiskey runner to boot, an' a *murderer* because he sent men to take my sister's baby."

Clifford took a step back like he'd been hit.

"Knowin' all of that an' seein' a lot of it firsthand, you'll see how I'm fightin' shy of you raisin' my nephew. My sister, God keep her, intended for her son to become a good man. I'm gonna make sure that happens."

Clifford shot her a stern look. "No, you're not."

"Mr. Clifford," Bass said before Rose could argue further, or perhaps shoot the man where he stood, "if you don't give that baby to this young woman, and I mean *right now*, I'm gonna arrange for a family reunion for you and your son. I can tell you plain, Judge Parker won't mind hanging a kidnapping father right alongside his murdering son. Are we clear?"

Clifford wilted almost immediately and gave orders to send for the baby.

Bass drove the buckboard that took them from the Clifford ranch. Rose sat beside him and cuddled her nephew in a baby blanket. She waited till they'd cleared the fenceline around the ranch before she broke down and cried.

Uncertain whether the tears were happy or sad, or might even be from the wound in her side, Bass didn't say anything. Women didn't always want a man to see their tears either. Sometimes it was best to just leave such things alone.

But when that baby smiled up at Rose, her tears went away in a heartbeat and she smiled back. Bass relaxed a little then, and he knew everything was going to be all right.

THE END

# What You Don't Learn In School

As I've gotten older, I've decided it's a shame how little we really get taught in school. I mean, I grew up in Oklahoma and I can't remember when I first heard of Bass Reeves. That acquaintance didn't happen in junior high school in Seminole, Oklahoma, though I do remember stories of William "Alfalfa Bill" Murray, the ninth governor of the state who called out the National Guard and argued with Texas regarding the bridge over the Red River.

And I didn't hear about Bass Reeves in high school, though I heard lots of stories about Bill Pickett, who grew up in Taylor, Texas. I grew up in the country and our heroes might not have been cowboys, but we certainly gave a lot of respect to guys who busted broncs and rode bulls.

Nope, I heard about Bass Reeves sometime later on my own. I'm a dual major, in English and History, and I read a lot. So somewhere in there, I tripped across the legendary U. S. Marshal all on my own. I've even seen the statue of Bass Reeves in Fort Smith, Arkansas.

He was an impressive guy, a man's man and a father, and someone who could toe the line and stand tall.

So I was thankful to get a chance to contribute to the legend, even though my story is—mostly—fiction. You see, my grandpa lived in Stringtown, Oklahoma, and my father was born there. When I started looking around for ideas for "Whiskey Road," I wanted to use my Oklahoma roots, something that I don't often get the chance to do. My grandpa, Melvin "Shorty" Odom, Senior, was a banty Irishman, who stood four foot ten inches tall. My father, Melvin Junior, stood five foot two. In my father's family, I'm practically a giant at five foot seven.

Shorty raised hogs and children, and my father did too. I grew up around pig pens, the stink of which never truly goes away, and I knew I would never raise them. I broke a lot of horses when I was still young enough to bounce, and I eat bacon with a vengeance.

I knew a lot of stories about those pioneer folks. My father's mother was descended from the Fountains and the Dickersons, two of the top ten worst outlaw families in the Territories and after statehood.

My pedigree is mixed, and I'm a country boy at heart, so people who read my science fiction and fantasy stuff will see this as a change-up. Getting to write this story and travel—in my imagination—the tall timber of land my grandpa and great-grandpa knew in their lives was a nice change of pace.

I hope you enjoy the adventure!

**MEL ODOM** - grew up in southeastern Oklahoma, where diehard country boys still eat possums and soft-shelled turtles, but now lives in Moore, Oklahoma, a wonderful town that unfortunately attracts Pecos Bill riding a twister on a regular basis. He's lived through hog raising and F-5 tornados, surely two of the most dangerous things in the world.

Over the last twenty-plus years, he's written dozens of novels in many different genres, including some based on television shows like *Buffy the Vampire Slayer* and novelizations of *Blade, Tomb Raider,* and *xXx.* He's trekked through deadly forests and braved the Sword Coast in the Forgotten Realms, and written adventures of bioroid detectives in Fantasy Flight's Android game.

He teaches in the Professional Writing program at the University of Oklahoma and writes all the time. He can be reached at mel@melodom.net, www.melodom.blogspot.com, @melodom on Twitter, and on Facebook.

His current military science fiction trilogy, *The Makaum War,* has been hitting bestseller lists.

# NO MASTER BUT DUTY

by Andrew Salmon

It was in that twilight instant when day and night hold equal sway over the land that Rain Crow rode up to the rough ranch house. The freedman's plot was twenty acres, mostly scrub brush bordered by a line of trees like a black saw blade against the purple sky west of Tahlequah near the Arkansas river before it crooked south to meet the Canadian. The small town of Witherell was an hour's ride.

He dismounted, the jingle of spurs and creak of leather loud in the silence. The rancher's sons would be making their way back to the ranch house soon. The odor of stew and biscuits reached Rain Crow as he led his horse to the tumbleweed wagon used to transport prisoners. With Kennedy and the chuck wagon over to Morehead with a busted axle, the smell of home cooking put a rumble in his belly and was a prelude to the noise and bluster of men after a hard day in the field and a night of ease before the sun brought tomorrow's cares.

Rain Crow was of medium height with a breadth of shoulders that dissuaded trouble. Black hair, an open face, he appeared more youthful than he was but the lines etched into his dry, burnished face whispered of other times and hard choices.

The porch door creaked when he opened it. The sound lost in the rumble of laughter from the kitchen at the end of the stark, narrow hallway. A smatter of voices rose up quickly as if to conceal the joyful sound. Rain Crow's spurs punctuated each stride as he made his way along the faded runner down the hallway.

"My posseman, I reckon."

Rain Crow recognized the voice of Bass Reeves as a hushed question was interjected and the silence that followed instantly on the heels of that simple statement deepened. A prompting grunt from Reeves encouraged

Crane Lemon to finish what he'd been saying before Crow's presence had been detected.

Not wanting to interrupt, Rain Crow stepped lightly across the doorsill but his appearance halted the flow of words again as Lemon flicked his gaze to the face of Rain Crow turned the color of tallow by the dying twilight.

Reeves sat a kitchen chair, his large frame relaxed back against the scarred wood, one long leg thrust out beneath the table, the boot between Crane Lemon and his wife. Elbows tight against the arm joints, Reeves conveyed attention along with ease. To encourage Lemon to take up his tale in the presence of a Cherokee, Reeves inclined his massive head slightly to indicate the covered plate Sissy Lemon had on the sideboard for Rain Crow's return.

Rain Crow nodded his thanks and turned to one side to manage the slim gap between the chair Reeves sat and the edge of the counter. He nodded his thanks again and set to. A negro kitchen had long lost its strangeness to him and he felt right at home despite the anxious glances the Lemons kept throwing at him.

"Go on now, sir," Reeves broke the unspoken silence. He was much different from the last time Rain Crow had seen him that afternoon. Reeves had changed out of his road clothes into his best blue suit and crisp white shirt. This meant they were going into town tonight and wouldn't wait for morning.

"I-It don' fall to me to pass judgment on where the white man come and go," Lemon said, haltingly. "Not much good come of that." He indicated the rifle Reeves had propped up against the stove. "Not so long ago, Cherokee'd lay the lash cross your back just for carryin' that Winchester. White man kill you dead. We keep to our own."

"Recountin' will do presently," replied Reeves and his teeth flashed white like tombstones in the long bramble of his greying moustache. "We'll leave the judgin' to folks specializin' in that. Night's comin' on."

Lemon was jolted by the words and sat up straight as if he were on the witness stand. "I seen the man you call Jim Hill." His words seemed to pick up speed. "Rode up the main road. Sure as you're sitting there, Marshal. No hurry, him."

"Loaded for bear?" asked Reeves.

"No, suh. Clothes on his back."

"Jack rabbity?"

"No, suh. Mighty calm looked like."

"Think, now. No trouble around these parts since you saw him?"

"No, suh."

"Quiet before, too?"

"Yes, suh."

Reeves raised a massive hand to scratch thoughtfully at the hair behind his right ear. "Well, that's somethin' anyhow."

A thoughtful silence descended on the shadowed kitchen. Reeves shifted one side of his mustache over and the wrinkles on the opposite side of his face undulated like a wave as he worked his jaw.

Rain Crow, hungry from the day's riding, had cleaned his plate by this time. Seeing this, Sissy Lemon thrust out of her seat to take the dish from his hands. He pretended he didn't see her stop short as if she were drawing near a grizzly and extended the plate to her.

"Thank you, kindly, ma'am."

"We'll trouble you no more," Reeves said. "We'll keep the wagon tucked behind the house until we're back with our man. Not like to be many travelin' at night, especially with rain comin' on."

Everyone in the kitchen was aware of the risk Reeves and his party posed to the freedmen farmers. The law was alien in the Indian Territory for the most part and scratching out a living aged one before his time. Everyone had a hand in something and neighbors might get nervous if they saw folks extending hospitality to a deputy US Marshal. This was why Reeves had delayed their arrival until sundown.

In the years Rain Crow had worked as posseman for Reeves he never knew the Marshal to blunder into a situation, putting his own life in jeopardy or that of anyone else. Rain Crow also knew that the idea Reeves had of collaring Hill and spiriting him out of town while folks were at their suppers was not going to come off that easy.

Reeves rose to his impressive six foot, two-inch height and looked down benignly on the Lemons who had followed him to their feet.

"I thank you for your hospitality," he said. "Rain Crow?"

The Indian placed the balled up napkin on the tabletop and joined Reeves as the Lemons preceded them to the front door. It was almost full dark by this point and the wagon loomed ghostly in the wan candlelight tracing them from the doorway.

"Let's get it round back," said Reeves. "It ain't getting any lighter."

"Sure thing," Rain Crow replied. "The sorrel?"

Reeves nodded. "We'll ride in high."

"Townsfolk don't like law. Runs contrary to arrangements with drifting, lawless skunks passing through. Can go hard for us."

"I know it," Reeves replied. "I reckon we can put hands on Hill presently, not have to spend the night. Spied him?"

"I did not. That is why I mention townsfolk. Ain't going to be no in and out job. Word is Hill lit out late afternoon, west, and not a soul knows where…least, they ain't saying."

Reeves considered this a moment. "He keep his room in town?"

"Yup."

"Ain't but one rooming house in Witherell. He be back. We be waitin'. We keep it as quiet as we can in the meanwhile."

"I hear you. Only that fine sorrel and them high clothes of yours, well, they tip your hand it's the law riding in."

"That's all right. Good to play it square. That bunch might have arranged themselves to shelter a fugitive in exchange for no trouble on the streets but that don't mean they going to cotton to the likes of Hill. They see we're to cart him away, they won't pay us no mind as we work."

"He riding along like Lemon says, they'll know he ain't got cohorts to make them pay for turning a blind eye. It could go like that."

"Glad to see the back of him, I expect."

The wagons tucked behind the Lemons' home and Kennedy left behind to try their hospitality, Reeves and Rain Crow turned their mounts towards Witherell.

"It bother you back there?" asked Reeves. "That pie-eyed skittishness of the Lemons?"

"Only so much my being in their home caused undue nerves. Many negro Cherokee freedmen stay in Territory even with trouble sometimes, with Seminoles mostly. Territory better for them than the United States. Here they own business, earn living, most equal with full blood Cherokee. The Lemons? I do not know who was their Cherokee master. Nothing I can do, is there?"

"You're wrong about that. We can uphold the law; see they get a fair chance at it."

"Bringing in Jim Hill will make that much of a difference?"

"If not to them direct, then folk like them. Been my experience people want to live in peace as much as the lost want to tear it down."

They could see the lights of Witherell through the tree branches clacking in the wind that had picked up. Witherell was laid out like a bent horseshoe, the open end facing west. Reeves and Rain Crow approached from the southeast where a side street curled around onto Main Street, leading to the livery and the hotel. The next bend would get them into town but before they reached it, gunshots cracked off and the thud of hoofs at a gallop snapped Reeves and Rain Crow alert.

A quick assessment eased their minds as they determined that the noise was distant, from the west while they rode in from the east. A chorus of shouts and yells told them that whatever was brewing, the townsfolk had been yanked from their suppers, choosing to satisfy their curiosity over their bellies.

"Split up," Reeves directed. "I'll ride straight in, you swing in wide. When we got the play, we'll work it close. And I don't want Hill getting by us into the forest because we bunched."

Rain Crow broke off, cutting through an opening in the post oak and elm trees lining the road. The glow from the town was enough for him to see by and he disappeared with the crack of branches and creak of saddled leather. Reeves didn't spare him a look. He'd ridden with Rain Crow before and the man knew his work. Urging his horse to a trot, Reeves continued up the center of the main road.

The noise from the townsfolk increased, doors slammed and boots thundered on the boardwalk. Reeves could see them now, men and women exchanging curious, expectant glances as they rushed towards the source of the excitement, kicking up clouds of dust.

Coming into town, Reeves lost the stars and couldn't tell if this was due to the lights in every window or clouds from the approaching storm. When he guided his sorrel off the main road between the rear end of a restaurant and the side of the general store, a gust of wind came up suddenly to dispel the cloying warmth from the kitchen and tug at the sleeves of his suit. He felt his hat start to go and clamped one hand down on it to keep it in place. The wind sealed it for him. Rain was coming and it would be upon the town sooner rather than later.

Yelling punctuated by the odd pistol shot still resounded up ahead, which was why Reeves had altered his entry to the town. With their blood up, they would just as soon shoot at a strange negro appearing suddenly out of the swirling dust as they would at the evening sky so caution was needed.

Through the alley up ahead, Reeves saw the mass of people shifting nervously. He could not see what had drawn their attention as yet.

The wind picked up and so did the dust. The word went out to take the gathering inside and the street cleared as Reeves prepared to guide his horse up the alley. Now that he could approach unchallenged, he abandoned the alley and returned to the main road.

He rounded the corner of the Ace High saloon and made for the tie-rail in front. A dusty form took shape with a blast of wind. It was a dead man tied hand and foot, twisted like a corkscrew, his arms pulled backwards over his head. Reeves took in the dirty form, torn, faded blue shirt and hide leggings dappled with dust over blood amidst the twigs and leaves caught in the folds and tears. He wore a fine gunbelt, tooled, the leather still sporting a sheen here and there beneath the dust.

The battered face of the man now drew the attention of Reeves. It was upturned with one eye swollen shut, the other like a cold marble turned to the heavens in the broad face with one prominent cheekbone smashed, mouth hanging open. Lines of scratches drew thin red lines along one cheek and neck, a thorn embedded behind one ear. The wind kicked up dust into swirling clouds and played with the dirt in the open mouth of the dead man, creating a miniature dust devil to swirl past the shattered, rotten teeth and off into the darkness.

Reeves studied the dead man with his piercing gaze, then climbed down and looped the sorrel's reins over the post. He crouched and examined the gunbelt. With one thick finger he traced a tear in the black leather and the clotted dust came away. The leather beneath the black dye was bright tan. Reeves dusted his hands together. He'd come for Jim Hill and now he had a dead Cherokee who'd been dragged behind a horse. Well, the answers were inside.

He stepped through the saloon doors into the cacophonous noise of the assembled men and women. Their excitement palpable. The wind at his back swung the doors shut with authority.

"Listen up, folks!" a man at the bar shouted over the din. "A moment of your attention, if you please."

The speaker was a tall gentleman, almost as tall as Reeves, but his height did not convey the same bearing for its slightness detracted from his appearance. No, it was his clothes that did the job for him. His well cut, black swallow-tail coat fitted him perfectly, his paisley vest snug around his trim torso. Fawn trousers with razor sharp creases completed the image of the well-to-do businessman. A wide-brimmed, charcoal hat rested on the end of the bar at his elbow. A black mourning band around one upper arm mixed with the somber color of his coat and was not noticeable at first. The lanterns cast light over his form, sparking off the shine of his clean boots and tracing the grey strands in his short Van Dyke and at his temples. The lit cigar in his raised hand sent out a curling snake of smoke to mix with the grey cloud suffusing the room.

"All right!" roared the sheriff at his side. "Ben Sinclair's got something to say to y'all. Quiet down!"

Reeves didn't spare more than a glance for the thin, stooped-shouldered sheriff with his bald pate and tired gray eyes. The man standing between Sinclair and Sheriff Fogel, puffing his chest out and flashing a lop-sided, gap-toothed grin was Jim Hill. Lank, oily brown hair obscured his deep set green eyes and ragged eyebrows as he gazed insolently at Reeves and worked his unshaven chin this way and that.

Sinclair raised his hands to quiet the crowd and a semblance of silence was attained.

"It's been a long hunt," he said, his voice cultured, his tone commanding. "That dead Indian out there is not a pretty sight but he is a sight for sore eyes. We have Mr. John Poole to thank for that."

He gestured at Jim Hill for emphasis and Reeves laughed in his throat as a round of cheers and applause erupted. Reeves looked over the crowd; saw that Rain Crow had managed to insert himself into it without drawing attention as the crowd consisted of Indians, negroes and white men. They were ready to move if it came to that.

Sinclair raised his clean palms again. "We are in his debt. And the town of Witherell honors its obligations. Not only will Sheriff Fogel here see that Mr. Poole gets the reward offered for the bandit, Running Elk, but I shall personally double it by kicking in an additional $500! Thank you, Mr. Poole!"

The crowd burst into applause again. Reeves had heard enough. While the men and women clapped and shouted, their teeth flashing wetly in the flickering light, Reeves skirted along one edge of the crowd in the direction of Sheriff Fogel and the fugitive masquerading as Poole.

Hill saw Reeves first and paled noticeably, the idiotic grin sliding from his face. There was no recognition in Hill's reaction other than an instant knowledge that a lawman bore down on him. Fogel's next words sent a trickle of ice water down Hill's spine.

"Deputy Marshal Bass Reeves!" Fogel blurted, eyes like pie plates. "As sure as I'm standing here."

For eighteen years, Reeves had traveled through Indian Territory for Judge Parker. In that time, he'd never failed to exercise a writ. He was tenacious, inventive and intelligent. Outlaws respected him as much as they despised him. Attempts had been made on his life by those looking to make a name for themselves or to get him off their trails. These men were either in jail back at Fort Smith or underground. The jail, known as hell on the border by its former inhabitants, ensured rough going for Reeves as the men and women he hunted would do most anything to avoid going back there. And the reputation Reeves had earned for being relentless hampered him at times as those he trailed, sure he would ultimately run them to ground, were willing to try desperate means in escaping their fate.

"What yer seeing here is all stand up," Fogel added. "We got a right to protect our own."

"That's as may be," said Reeves, coming to stand with the trio at the bar. "And we will talk about it down the line." He locked his gaze on Rain Crow and the silent message to keep close watch on Jim Hill was passed. "Presently, I'd like a word in private. They a stock room back of this place?"

"Sure. Only can't it wait?" countered Fogel. "We're celebratin' here."

"Killin' a man?"

"It's not like that," Sinclair said. "That man out there is a thief. He has been robbing us blind for months."

Reeves ignored Sinclair. "Won't take but a minute, Sheriff."

"I reckon I can spare that for the likes of Bass Reeves." He jerked a long, thin thumb over his bony shoulder. "Back here'll do. Ace won't mind, seein' as it's you doing the askin'."

Reeves moved to follow Fogel and was surprised to see Sinclair join him. "Sheriff and me can handle this."

Sinclair adopted a dignified air. "Hardly. I will join you, Marshal."

"Suit yourself."

They withdrew to the stock room. They wound their way through the narrow, dim room heaped with casks on wooden shelves and piles of wood. The air was thick, heavy, redolent of mold and fermentation. Their passage stirred dust motes to the point it appeared the room smoldered. A tower of glass bottles stood in one corner and it was here they stopped.

"What's this all about, Reeves?" Sinclair demanded.

Reeves fixed him with a perplexed look, then turned his attention to Fogel. He withdrew a folded sheet of paper from the inside pocket of his suit jacket and extended it to the sheriff.

"That's an arrest warrant for Jim Hill," he explained. "The man you're toasting outside is Jim Hill."

"Poole?" said Sinclair. "There must be some mistake."

"As you can see, Sheriff, the writ is in order," Reeves continued. "Speak-

*"That's an arrest warrant for Jim Hill, the man you're toasting outside."*

ing my mind, I'm not opposed to Hill having a final taste as he'll be doing without where he's going. But I will take my man directly he's washed his tonsils. Let's be clear on that."

"You'll do nothing of the sort," said Sinclair. "Mr. Poole has done this town a great service. He's a hero!"

Reeves addressed Sinclair's comments. "A white spot on a bitin' hound don't change the nature of the beast. Hill is a murderer and a horse thief and I will bring him. Says dead or alive on that writ. Saying that, I don't cotton to killing a man as a means to simplifyin' a situation. He is going back at any rate. We'll see how she breaks down." The marshal returned his attention to Fogel. "Sheriff, can I count on your assistance with this duty?"

"Now, Marshal, you have to excuse Mr. Sinclair here as he's just recently buried his wife of many years."

"I do not need you to make excuses for me," Sinclair interrupted.

"May I count on you, Sheriff?" Reeves insisted.

Fogel flicked his nervous gaze to Sinclair but the gentleman bolted from the room.

"Ladies and gentlemen," roared Sinclair back at the bar. "There's a Deputy US Marshal seeking to haul Mr. Poole away to the hangman's noose! What say you to that? Will you stand for that?"

The gathered erupted in protest and a building fury began to color their movements as fists clenched at their sides, hands inched towards gun belts and epithets were heard through clenched teeth as a telling silence descended on the room. Rain Crow pushed his way through the crowd in the direction of Hill should the man choose to bolt. The crowd crept closer to the bar and every eye took on a predatory gleam.

Reeves and Fogel returned hurriedly and curses were flung at the Marshal who gave no response to them. He towered over the men, his cross-draw gunbelts on display, the pistols within easy reach. In his dark blue suit and black Stetson, he cut an imposing figure. Keeping his features neutral, he surveyed the crowd appraisingly, eyes catching and holding the intense stares directed at him. He faced farmers and merchants not hardened killers but their blood was up and they were armed and that was a fool's combination.

Taking his cue from Sinclair, Sheriff Fogel attempted to defuse the situation. "What we have here is a simple misunderstanding. Marshal Reeves is after a law-breaking snake and has confused Poole for that man. Settle down, folks, and we'll straighten her out."

This calmed the crowd to a certain extent, tense shoulders relaxed as glances were cast about. The glares at Reeves were still white hot however. The law and lawmen meant trouble in the Territory. Many towns offered outlaws asylum in exchange for immunity from attack. A Marshal in town for any length of time was a risk to that arrangement. It would bring trouble if the Marshal stayed the night. Following Fogel's calming words, the crowd settled slightly. Hill lost the cornered rat look stitched into his face since Reeves had made his presence known and the rattlesnake grin stretched his bloodless lips again.

Sinclair couldn't keep a condescending look of triumph off his face. "You see, Marshal, a simple case of mistaken identity. That's all. Ace! Drinks all around! We're celebrating!"

This went a long way to restoring the festive spirit of the crowd though baleful looks were still cast at Reeves. Rain Crow caught his eye and the Marshal shook his head a fraction. With the blood of a fresh kill in their nostrils, it was not time to force the matter with Hill. Doing so would touch off a shooting match and who knew how many would fall.

"Won't you join us is a glass," Sinclair offered magnanimously. "This is a great day for Witherell. Unless you want to try shooting it out with your prisoner in tow."

Reeves stared down at Hill a moment, saw the minute cringe in the outlaw's posture and the grin freeze a moment, then turned to Sinclair, angling his head to one side as he considered the turn of events. "I could shoot you."

Sinclair opened his coat. "I am unarmed."

"You and that bartender about the only ones in here unheeled," said Reeves. "Not so sure about the barkeep."

Sinclair's laughter was hollow, feigned. "I used to carry a firearm, for pheasants and such and had a good hand for it. Until I broke that hand years ago and wasn't able to hit a damned thing after that."

Reeves grinned but the mirth did not reach his eyes. "With shooting out of it, and a drink on the offering. Thank you, kindly. Don't mind if I do."

"That's the spirit!" Sinclair nodded quickly in satisfaction and pounded on the bar. "Ace! Dry throats down here!"

The proprietor of the establishment stepped lively and whiskey went around.

"Can't win 'em all, eh, nigger?" offered Hill, emboldened by his protectors and the liquor in his gut. "Me being the hero of the hour, I take no offense as I knows yer kind is saddled with little in the way of brains."

Reeves was not going to fall for Hill's childish attempt to rattle him.

He agreed to the drink because he was late to the show and needed to get caught up on what he'd missed.

"Let's hear more about Running Elk," Reeves said to Sheriff Fogel. "What got him dead in the dust outside?"

"You name it," replied Fogel. "Started out taking a head or two from the surrounding ranches. Got under our skin but not enough to turn every hand agin him. Turned highwayman after that but no one got killed, just roughed a little. We lit out after him but being Cherokee Indian, we didn't get nowheres with that. It was when he, and a small band of the same ilk, took the payroll from Mr. Sinclair's sawmill. That's what swung it. Most of the townsfolk make their living on account of the mill. After that, we hunted him hard. But Running Elk wouldn't fall easy. Stuck back to his thievin' ways. Took to stealing from homes right here in town, when he wasn't laying in wait for road travelers."

"Sounds a right nasty piece of work," said Reeves. "You have evidence against him? Statements from his victims? Judge Parker would appreciate seeing them."

"Can't say as I do. We just knowed it was him. Not many secrets in a town this size."

"We bagged the right scoundrel," added Sinclair. "I've been saying it all along and I'll stake my reputation on that."

Reeves took this in stride. "How does a snake like Hill here enter into it?"

"Why you old coon!" blurted Hill. "Keep on like thet an I'm likely to lose my forgivin' air."

Reeves leaned in close and hissed. "Shut your head or I'll shut it for you. Mind me, boy!"

Hill whipped his head around, fury twisting his mouth. Until he caught the look in the eyes of Reeves and his bravado turned to dust. He turned to look straight ahead, his hand turning his glass like a nervous safecracker working a dial, an insolent expression on his ferret face.

"See here, Reeves," Sinclair began.

"You did a fine job keeping the crowd off its hind legs after Mr. Sinclair here ran his mouth," Reeves interrupted, addressing Fogel. "I went along because there's been enough killing tonight. But if you think I've been buffaloed by what you done, think again."

"Now you listen, and listen good," said Sinclair. "Mr. Poole here is this town's saviour. And this town exists because of Sinclair Lumber. He got the rat out of our walls and he is free to stay here as long as he wishes. Any attempt to arrest him will be resisted. Understand that, Marshal!"

"Sheriff?" prompted Reeves.

Fogel stared down into his whiskey.

"All right, then," said Reeves. "We've laid our cards on the table and that's progress of a sort. Sheriff Fogel, Mr. Sinclair, I bid you good evening."

With that, Reeves made for the door. A boom of thunder followed by the hiss of rain announced the arrival of the expected storm. He was almost at the door when Hill's words reached him.

"Ladies and gents!" shouted Hill, venom in every word, "I give ya Marshal Reeves! He come in an uppity nigger looking to stir up trouble, he leaves right settled thanks to the Sheriff and Mr. Sinclair!"

Reeves never broke stride as he left the saloon.

Rain Crow joined Reeves at the Newgate Hotel an hour later. Reeves had taken the room right after the saloon while Rain Crow had mingled with the crowd to learn what he can before returning to the room he'd rented yesterday when he'd first ridden into town.

"Hill stuck good?" asked Reeves.

"Dug in like tick. Fogel, Sinclair toast him to beat the band."

Reeves snorted, his eyes closed as he reclined against the iron bed frame. His massive hands were curled in his lap like dead crabs.

"What do we do now?"

"We check out their story."

"Check what?" Rain Crow went to stand at the window and gaze down at the livery. Reeves had the window open six inches despite the slashing rain and cold wind that found its way across the sill. He had chosen the room because it overlooked the stable and, being a light sleeper, he'd hear if Hill tried to walk his horse out under cover of the storm. Reeves and Rain Crow couldn't watch him day and night. "We have seen dead Cherokee. We have seen celebratin'. We have seen town singin' Hill's praises."

"Ain't enough."

"What more you need?"

"We know who we up against," began Reeves. "Men like Hill are of a breed. Hard men whose only look out is themselves. Been in and out of jail since they first rode that trail, left bodies and tormented souls behind them on their way to ruin. Hill don't know any other way."

"You don't think he killed Running Elk?"

"Ain't going that far yet. I'm fixed on why he'd do it just now. Man takes a big risk every time he aims a pistol at a body. Hill's not the kind to gamble with those odds."

"Money?"

"His kind take what they want by any means. They don't earn it honest from someone else."

"I not follow path of your words."

"Hill's kind feed off the land and the backs of others. One place's as good as another so long as theys folks to rob. This'un came here direct out of Fort Smith, ain't touched the spreads on the trail in. We heard that from Lemon. A fella gets to asking why Hill would bypass easy pickings to come here to bet his life on gun work."

Rain Crow grinned. "You not think he just doin' duty?"

Reeves chuckled. "I don't know what he was doing but I aim to find out."

Rain Crow's expression grew serious. "We in for it, looks like. They not hand 'em over, Marshal. He's their number one boy."

"And that's how we'll go at it," replied Reeves. Rain Crow shook his head, confused. Reeves continued. "We'll sleep on it some as we ain't playing with a full deck at the moment. We going to find out about this Running Elk tomorrow."

The morning came clear and bright with a freshness courtesy of the rain the night before. Rain Crow had been up before first light to determine their best route out of town so as not to be seen leaving by the townsfolk. In the wake of the public humiliation of the previous night, he feared their being seen heading out of town like a pair of whipped pups would erase any shred of credibility they had with the town of Witherell.

Reeves was having none of that. "We go straight down the main street," he said over his morning coffee. "As our departin' is part of our job, we go heads high. We answer to no man here. Judge Parker wants to tear a strip off me, I'll hang my head if I'm deserving of his wrath. The Lord Almighty can do with me as He pleases. Those are the only two I bow to. Let's git. We need a line on the nearest Cherokee lighthorsemen if we're going to put the irons on Jim Hill sooner rather than later."

Their presence was noted before they managed to descend the hotel steps to the street. Reeves had exchanged the fine suit he'd worn the day before for an old brown jacket and ragged canvas trousers. Rain Crow wore stout hide leggings and a tattered, black suit coat.

The negro stable owner, whose name was Nelson, caught their intent and disappeared into the black maw of the livery, grey as a tomb in the dawn. The other townsfolk could be seen whispering, their heads turning, leaning in towards one another conspiratorially as each stopped on their way to take in the great Bass Reeves leaving town with his tail between his legs.

Nelson led their horses out minutes later, saddled and ready. Reeves and Rain Crow checked the straps as a matter of course while the horses shifted in the mud. Reeves slid his Winchester into its scabbard and mounted, paying the curious no mind. He thanked Nelson and flipped him a shiny silver dollar as a token of appreciation. They'd be back when their work was done but he didn't tell Nelson that. Witherell being a small town, Reeves didn't want everyone knowing his business. Over the years more than one outlaw had tried to shoot him down or lie in wait and there was no advantage in the town of Witherell knowing his comings and goings beforehand. It seemed a small risk as Nelson had the look of someone who'd be liquored up by noon and snore the afternoon away.

Rain Crow was mounted and ready and they rode out of town in search of the lighthorsemen.

The Cherokee farmed north, spreading out from the Boston Mountains, while the Canadian District in the south was allotted for the freedmen like Lemon. The lighthorsemen tended to patrol closer to the Cherokee spreads but many of the Cherokee freedmen had joined since the war to protect the negroes who had used their Cherokee blood to receive land. Although they did not have the authority to arrest white men, the lighthorsemen were granted judgment over Indian, freedmen and negro affairs and had to rely on dissuading drifters, squatters and outlaws without officially detaining them. Witherell lay between the two sections of the Territory so it was a safe bet riding in any direction would bring results if time was not an issue. Reeves had ridden with the Indian Defense Forces during the war so he knew the ways into to the Territory that didn't draw a lot of unwanted attention. Heading northeast towards the Arkansas border was their best bet. The government didn't abide negro settlers in Indian Territory and turned a blind eye to the poor whites, thieves and otherwise, squatting on any parcel of land in the Territory they fancied, the freedmen allotments especially. So the lighthorsemen he needed to find would most likely ride close to the border to spot squatters before they took root. North and east it was and Reeves hoped they wouldn't have to get around the Ozarks. If so, they wouldn't make it back before sunup the next day and he was loath to leave Hill unwatched for so long.

Their luck held. Just before midday, a Cherokee fishing Vine Creek told them a band of lighthorsemen had passed him not more than an hour ago. The leader, so he said, had been a big man with one arm. Reeves had smiled at that and thanked the man.

They caught up to the lighthorsemen in a clearing less than an hour later after some hard riding. The sun was up, burnishing the colored leaves and casting an unusual autumnal warmth across their shoulders. The lighthorsemen had coffee on and sprawled around their campfire, chatting loosely.

Reeves went right up the leader who sat, bare-chested in the sun. The man was full-blooded Cherokee, his hair snow white, his broad face wrinkled and seamed by the endless kneading of the sun. His broad chest rose and fell evenly, one muscled arm clasped to his chest as he sat cross-legged. The other extended from the red cannonball of his left shoulder to end at the elbow with the white, puckered flesh where the amputation had occurred following the Battle of Pea Ridge

"Brown Wolf, you old rascal!" said Reeves, climbing down off his horse. "How've the years been treating you?"

At the sound of the Marshal's voice, Brown Wolf snapped open his eyes and a flash of gums dotted here and there with the odd blackened tooth greeted the words. He sprang to his feet with the energy of the man a third of his sixty-three years and clasped the hand of Bass Reeves. So pleased was Brown Wolf to see his old friend that he lost his English and rattled off a string of Cherokee. Reeves smiled and answered back in Wolf's native tongue though not as smoothly. Reeves was fluent in Muskogee but his Cherokee was somewhat lacking.

The three men sat cross-legged upon the grass to speak of old times and long rides before Reeves brought up Jim Hill and any problems that had been reported concerning the outlaw. He did not show Brown Wolf the writ for the Cherokee could no more read it than Reeves.

"We add our voice to the others who speak no ill of him," said Brown Wolf. "The name Jim Hill has not reached our ears. No trouble has been reported with this man as the cause."

"He's using the moniker of John Poole in town."

Brown Wolf paused, thinking, then shook his head.

"Then that's settled in my mind," said Reeves. "What harms the

Cherokee besides the white squatters?"

"Now that is a question with many answers. I need not tell you of the outlaws and thieves for of these you know as much as I. The freedmen suffer at Indian hands as well and there are some on the Council who would deny them their Cherokee blood. Squabbles and claims enough to harden the heart. Like the nimble spider, we must glide carefully along the thin strand of justice."

"Don't forget Sinclair, old man," said a deep voice behind the three men.

"Moz!" shouted Reeves, a grin stretching his lips as he rose to his feet to great his old friend.

His name was Mozart Sims and, along with Bass Reeves, had served in the Indian tribal police in their youth after fleeing their masters to find sanctuary with the Five Civilized Tribes. Reeves and Sims were polar opposites. Whereas Reeves was tall and broad, Sims was stout as a cedar fencepost and as solid in his well-worn brown tweed shirt and pants. Sims was short, almost completely bald, the remaining hair at his temples dusted with gray.

"What's this about Sinclair?" asked Reeves after they'd expressed their pleasure at meeting up after so long and sat comfortably on the grass.

Sims lit a cigar and puffed hungrily before leaning back to brace himself on one elbow. "Lot of freedmen losing their allotments trying to live honest these days. If it ain't some Cherokee thinking the black man is still their property, it's the squatters and raiders. You know how it is out here, Bass. Whatever the cause, ol' Sinclair is stepping in to buy up freedmen land as fast as they have to get shed of it. Naming his price along the way."

"Expanding his timber interests," said Reeves.

"So you met 'im already. That's good. He'll own half the Territory before long, then sell it back to us a tree at a time. His wife not only took his name, she also left him her Jennings money. Man's so rich he doesn't know where to put it all."

The Jennings family was one of the richest in the United States, having amassed their fortune in shipping and rail.

"He on the square?"

"Far as anyone can prove, he is," said Brown Wolf. "Just bitter talk by those who lost their spreads mostly."

"I need to know about Running Elk."

At the name, Brown Wolf balled his remaining hand into a fist and pounded it against his thigh.

"What about him?" asked Sims.

"Killed last night outside Witherell by Jim Hill. They crowned Hill for it and, lest I can discredit him before the town, I'll have a dickens of a time prying him out of their hands. I need to know if this Running Elk was everything they're claiming he was. Man was killed without a hearing. I have my concerns about the charges."

Sims blew out a plume of cigar smoke. "If they were calling him a liar a thief and a murderer, they hit the nail on the head."

"Brown Wolf?"

Reeves watched his friend's face harden. "Running Elk was a disgrace to the Cherokee. Filled with hate and vengeance he stole, took the wives of others, lied against his brothers, drew blood without a second thought. There was no good in him and we drove him out. So he became an outlaw. We have hunted him as well for he preys on everyone in the Territory."

"It's been said he was robbing the people of Witherell though no one can claim to have witnessed him in the act."

"In the town, you say?" said Brown Wolf.

Reeves nodded.

"Seems he's gotten bold of late," observed Sims. "Running Elk started out as more of what's-to-hand thief. And he liked his privacy for his other needs, if you take my meaning. He sold land out from under freedmen. Indian or white, made no difference. Always with a sure getaway, mind. Not like him to work a town and bring a passel of men down on him. He liked the isolation of the farms."

Reeves shook his head as he considered what his friends had told him. "I'll admit I'm vexed by these reports. I had hoped to discredit Hill with his admirers and dimming the light they throwing on him in the hopes they'd turn on him and give him up. It was that or a gunplay and that's no sure bet with every hand turned against me. Sending word to Fort Smith would take too long and give Hill the chance to wriggle out from under."

"I am sorry we cannot offer help in this," said Brown Bear.

Sims smiled and, with a wink at Reeves, addressed Brown Bear. "Speak for yourself, old man. Some of us are still full o' beans."

Brown Bear did not miss a beat and replied, dryly. "Today is my last ride and it is pleasing to me to say goodbye to Mozart Sims when we return while the sun is in the sky."

The men laughed, then Reeves added. "They putting you out to pasture, Brown Bear? That's a sad thing to hear."

"It'll be our turn sooner rather than later, I reckon," said Sims. "Brown Bear's got a spread. He's gonna be a one-armed farmer."

The talk continued pleasantly for a few more minutes. Then Reeves

*"Seems Running Elk's gotten bold of late."*

exchanged a look with Rain Crow. "Best be at it. Hill won't keep."

The men stood and Reeves expressed his thanks for their help. Final words were exchanged. He and Rain Crow mounted up.

Reeves and Rain Crow turned more heads on the ride back into Witherell than they had heading out. The sun was starting to dip, turning the west side of each dwelling molten and it was low enough that the townsfolk had to raise their hands up or angle their hats to block the glare as the lawmen kicked their tired mounts in the direction of Nelson's.

With the horses seen to, Reeves and Rain Crow knocked the trail dust from their clothes then returned to their rooms. They were back on the street minutes later and split up. Rain Crow to find Jim Hill while Reeves headed over to the general store.

The townsfolk made a show of continuing on their way to mask the truth that they had stopped to gawk at the Marshal they thought they were shed of. Two of them did not try to hide their disdain. A white man and a negro who were not unfamiliar to Bass Reeves. They were Ed Bennett and Tim Hemp respectively. The Indian Territory was lawless for the most part and illicit activity was the stock and trade of these men. Putting their affairs on hold for a Marshal did not sit well with them. Staying the course was fine in the short term but it was their conclusion that Reeves had outstayed his welcome in Witherell.

Reeves caught their glares from the corner of his eye. He employed his prodigious memory to recall what he knew of them as he stepped up onto the boardwalk in front of Henderson's store. A cluttered jumble, the store was abundant in blankets, flour sacks, dried goods and tools. If these had been placed about the store with any attention paid to planning beforehand, Reeves made no sense of it. A thousand odors assailed the nostrils carried on currents of dust and stale air.

"Evenin', Marshal," said Henderson in a reedy voice. Gus Henderson was a short, wiry man with a mane of swept back blonde hair, sky blue eyes too big for his head and a mouth so small and white it looked like he'd been born without one.

"How long you owned this establishment—if you don't mind my asking?"

"Been here nine year, I reckon."

The answer satisfied Reeves who nodded curtly before continuing. "Running Elk worry your mind?"

"Not anymore," replied Henderson, laughing at his joke. The cold look

Reeves gave him strangled his mirth. "That son of a coyote? Gave us all fits he did."

"Ever stuck you up?"

"You mean in the daylight?"

Reeves nodded.

"Naw. His kind just as soon have at you when your back's turned."

"Night job, then?"

"You betcha. Mostly grub and blankets. Guns're locked up yonder." He stabbed a long finger at a glass cabinet against the far wall. Rifles, pistols, hunting knives gave off a dulled sheen in the windowless, shadowed corner of the store. "This close to the hotel, he'd bring half the town down on his head if they broke that glass so he steered clear."

Reeves gave the case a quick appraisal, then went on. "So you never saw Running Elk steal anything?"

"No, sir. Was the Sheriff put us wise to Running Elk. But I know the type anyhow. Came in here, big as you please one mornin'. Watched him careful, I did."

"Only he didn't steal anything."

Henderson chewed the inside of one cheek as he shook his head. "I watched him. He drifted over to that cabinet and I could see the look in his eye. The savage had murder in his heart."

"Store busy that time?"asked Reeves.

"No. We was alone."

"Why didn't he slit your throat, then help himself?"

Henderson's mouth fell open and his eyes looked about ready to fall out of his head at the thought. He recovered quickly and a sneer pulled at one side of his mouth, revealing teeth like kernels of corn, as he reached behind the counter and came up with a shotgun.

"He might'a tried but that's as far it would have gone."

Reeves gave him a look of assurance and Henderson returned the weapon to its place of concealment. When he straightened up he found Reeves admiring the gun belts hanging from wall pegs.

"These are mighty fine," Reeves said. "I'm partial to the Mexican loop, the top notch."

"Double drop loop buscadero?"

"That's the one. Got anything like that?"

Henderson shook his head.

"Seen anyone in town sporting such a belt?"

"No, sir. I'd have noticed as I have a penchant for firearms." Sudden realization came to Henderson. "You're talking about the belt that theivin' Indian was sportin', ain't ya?"

"He's a thief, right?" said Reeves. "If he didn't buy it here nor steal it, maybe someone in town had such a belt. Some evidence against Running Elk will sure help my report back to Fort Smith on the matter of the killing."

"Running Elk was a thief, no question of that. Most likely stole the belt somewheres. Lots of folks settling or passing through the Territory—all kinds—rich and poor alike, Indian and negro. All kinds. He stole it somewheres, that's certain."

"Thank you kindly for your time," Reeves said, setting his wide-brimmed hat on his head.

It took all of fifteen minutes for him to get similar answers from the other proprietors. Reeves considered they might all be reticent with information as a matter of course, seeing as he was a lawman and this was rough country. But it was in their best interests for him to leave town. Seemed more likely they'd fill his head with whatever he needed to hear if it got him gone that much sooner. The common thread was their unwavering trust in the judgment of Sheriff Fogel.

As he stepped down into the street from the wagonworks, he saw Rain Crow coming out of Nelson's. The Cherokee spotted Reeves and joined him.

"Hill?" Reeves asked.

"Marshal!" called out a voice behind them before Rain Crow could reply. It was Sheriff Fogel who shuffled up to them. "Word has it you boys were still in town though I have to say I doubt what my eyes are showing me. We thought you two were gone for good this morning."

Reeves regarded the Sheriff frankly. "There's business needs tending. I thought I made it clear I wasn't leaving without Hill. Where is he?"

"I can't rightly say."

"Toast of the town only last night and now no one's seen him?"

"We went at it pretty hard last night, celebratin'. Long into the night to boot. My head's swole up like I been snakebit. I reckon half the town's still got a sore head even now. Enough to give ol' Nelson a run for his money."

"I don't doubt it," said Reeves. "Where's the man holds your leash?"

Fogel grimaced at the insult but had had long practice absorbing scorn and answered regardless. "Since his wife passed, Mr. Sinclair's thrown himself into his work. Seeing to the new mills he's building, buying up land, and burning the midnight oil at the local mill. Back and forth to Arkansas every other week. Everywhere at once since the funeral. Hard work's good for what ails you, they say. Takes his mind off his loss as he tells it. Still it was that, what do you call, irony with Mrs. Sinclair. What with her not wanting anything to do with Witherell, then passing peaceful in her sleep so quick after getting here."

"Has a sawbones had a look at Running Elk? Cause of death got to go in my report. And I'd like to know if it was Hill's bullet or the drag through the countryside that did him in."

"Doc Evans pulled up stakes more 'n year ago," Fogel replied. "Folks rely on shamans and home remedies ever since."

Reeves had heard enough of Fogel's blather and turned to his posseman, prompting, "Rain Crow?"

"No sign of Hill, Marshal," he replied, then motioned with his head over one shoulder. "His horse is stabled. It has not been ridden recently."

"Nelson add anything?"

"He is still climbing out of the jug beside his bed."

"He's the last one I got to question about Running Elk. So far, no one in town can swear he was the cause of all their troubles."

"The Indian was no good," observed Fogel.

"You hear me saying Running Elk didn't commit every one of those robberies? I know what he was. What I'm saying is that no one can swear to seeing him do it. Except..."

"Land sakes! It's murder! Help!"

The three men whipped their heads around to see Nelson staggering drunkenly out of the stable entrance. Eyes wide, arms outstretched as though fending off invisible assailants, the man moved as fast as his spindly legs could carry him. The mud tripped him up and he sprawled, flailing in his intoxication and panic. A crowd began to gather around the three lawmen.

"What's this?" asked Fogel. "Your man was just in there!"

Reeves, Rain Crow and Fogel crossed the street at a run. Reeves helped Nelson to his feet. "What about this hollerin'."

"Murder!" Nelson sputtered.

Fogel put his hands on his hips and bent down to look in the stable owner in the eye. "Nelson ol' boy, you're drunk. You got to calm down."

Reeves took the old man by the shoulders and gave him a shake. "Tell it!"

"In there, suh!" Nelson managed his eyes wide as he met the calm gaze of Reeves. "Killed to death! Lord! They'll think I done it."

Rain Crow hurried inside and his voice was heard calling soon after.

"In here, Marshal!"

Reeves passed Nelson to Fogel and rushed inside to find his posseman and took in the scene.

"Damn it to hell!" spat Reeves.

He knelt to examine the body of Jim Hill. The dead man lay on his back in the hay trough. Dark blood ran the length of his checkered shirt from the long hunting knife thrust up between his ribs. There was blood on the straw. Hill's legs bent slight to fit the short length of the trough were mostly covered by hay. The pitchfork Nelson had been using lay a few feet away where the man had tossed it in his fright. It was clear that Nelson was spreading the grass for the horses from the trough and had stumbled upon the body someone had gone to considerable lengths to conceal.

"Cherokee knife, Marshal," said Rain Crow. "Kana'ti dagger. Beaver tail handle."

Fogel had joined them by this time and stood there, staring down at the murdered man, one finger sawing across his chin. The sound of insistent voices reached them from outside and Fogel turned in the doorway to prevent the townsfolk from entering.

"Let us do our work, folks," he said.

"There's a dead man in there or has Nelson gone loco?"

"Nelson told it true. Sure as shootin'."

An anxious shudder seemed to work through the crowd.

"You heard the Sheriff!" an angry voice rose above the others. "And that redskin with Reeves just came out of there not two minutes ago. Seen it with my own eyes!"

"Now don't talk foolish," said Fogel. "The Indian had no reason to kill Poole."

"Poole!" the name was taken up by the crowd. The man who had accused Rain Crow shouted over the crowd. "That's Frank Poole murdered in there? Those two have had it in for him since they rode into town."

Reeves followed the exchange outside as he and Rain Crown examined the body of Jim Hill. At one point he threw a glance past the Sheriff and identified the agitator in the crowd and confirmed it was Ed Bennett though the man held his tan duster tight and had his wide-brimmed black hat pulled low, one of two men he'd seen watching him earlier in the day. They'd been looking for any excuse to eliminate the law from Witherell and they'd just found it. The crowd took on a threatening tone, violence was imminent. He and Rain Crow had seconds to act.

"Time to go," he said, calmly.

Rain Crow understood immediately and rose to his feet, a hand on the butt of his revolver.

They couldn't risk time saddling the horses with the crowd beginning to push forward.

"Out the back! Before they hit on it," urged Reeves.

"I see 'em!" roared Bennett. "Theys runnin'!"

"Now hold on," was all Fogel could manage before he was shoved roughly to one side and a pistol cracked. The bullet whizzed into the hay bales stacked along the far wall. The lawnmen didn't wait for another.

Running full out, Reeves and Rain Crow reached the door at the opposite end of the stable and burst through into the early twilight.

"Don't let 'em get away!"

More shots echoed in the expanse of the stable. The horses whinnied and banged nervously against their stalls at the sound.

There was a quick stream running behind the stables that Nelson used to water the horses. Beyond that was a stand of red cedar. Reeves and Rain Crow splashed down into the shallow water and risked turned ankles sloshing across the rock bed. The mud on the far bank slowed them momentarily as their legs churned. Over the sound of the water, they heard boots scrape across gravel behind them. Part of the mob had circled around the building while those inside were hampered by the narrow door.

Shots lanced past them to slap the leaves and branches of the trees they were making for. Reeves and Rain Crow returned fire wildly as they were out in the open and did not have the luxury of standing and aiming. They fired instead to slow the pursuit and gain the quick seconds they needed to reach the cover of the trees.

They were almost there when Rain Crow cut to one side to avoid a boulder skirted with a patch of hawthorn with long thorns. The motion put him directly behind Reeves for an instant as a rifle cracked and he took the bullet meant for Reeves almost dead center in his back. His momentum carried him forward a few more stumbling steps before he pitched headlong at the edge of the trees.

Reeves had heard the impact and knew what it meant. Diving behind a fallen tree, he used the trunk for cover as he took deliberate aim at Bennett in the lead with his cronies and fired three well-placed shots. He didn't stop to see if he had hit his targets—he knew he had.

Shrieks of pain reached his ears and these were mingled with cries of caution as the mob floundered uncertainly for the moment.

Reeves took advantage of the confusion to get to Rain Crow and haul him behind the protection of the downed tree.

Rain Crow's face was ashen, droplets of blood dappled his lips and chin with each breath. The droplets grew in size. The man's chest bore a ragged hole, his shirt a mess of spreading blood, dirt and twigs from the fall. Shot through, Rain Crow was done for.

He saw the truth of his situation in the eyes of Reeves. The gun was still in his hand and Rain Crow raised it up to his chest, his eyes locked on the Marshal's. He nodded curtly.

Reeves understood and placed his palm on the top of Rain Crow's head as if administering a last benediction.

"I'll make it worthwhile," said Reeves as more shots began to pepper the woods around them. The mob had re-discovered their courage. "Rest easy."

Heart turned to stone; Reeves left his friend and moved deeper into the woods. The voices behind him grew louder as the crowd pressed forward. The ground was loamy and soft, uneven and the going was slow. Each step unleashed scuttling insects and the earthy smell of the grave. Branches whipped at him, his breathing was loud in his ears and he cursed the handful of grouse who took to the air at his approach to reveal his position.

The crack of Rain Crow's revolver sounded, followed by surprised yelps and cries of pain. Reeves tracked the sound of that pistol until it was smothered by a volley of shots. The excited whoops that followed told him that Rain Crow had bought him all the time he could.

Seething, Reeves fought to remain clear-headed. Branches snapped faintly behind him. The mob was after fresh game. They expected him to run like a rabbit, seeking the safety of distance with them hot on his heels until they ran him to ground.

Reeves was not going to oblige.

He paused to study the terrain. The thrashing of the slender branches as the twilight breeze toyed with a holly thicket told him there must be a clearing on the other side of it. He veered left sharply and disappeared into the foliage there. Pushing through to the trees beyond, he cut back towards Witherell and the stable.

He needed a horse.

The sky had begun to darken when he returned to the stable. Gun drawn, Reeves inched along the worn wood of one wall, careful to avoid making any sound as he stepped lightly across the loose pebbles. Through the gaps in the warped boards, he heard Sheriff Fogel muttering to himself as he brushed at his clothing. Knowing the damned Sheriff would talk the ears off anyone who was with him as he aired his complaints, Reeves concluded that the man was alone. Still, he rounded the corner of the doorway with his gun up and aimed.

He saw Fogel swiping at his hat that had been bent out of shape with the rough handling he'd received at the hands of the incensed townsfolk.

Experience had taught Reeves to never take anything for granted. "You alone?" he asked when the sound of his boots in the dirt made Fogel forget his hat and look up into the barrel of the Colt Peacemaker Reeves had leveled at him. The eyes of Fogel widened and he nodded dumbly.

Reeves holstered his gun and began to saddle his sorrel, making sure the Winchester was still in the scabbard.

"Overpowered me," complained Fogel. "Tossed me aside like a sorry hound. Ten years I been among 'em and I suffer such ill treatment."

Reeves worked quickly, ignoring Fogel. He got the saddled cinched and led the horse out of the stall.

He heard the click of a revolver being cocked behind him.

Reeves spun around to see Fogel pointing a gun at him. There was a haunted look in the Sheriff's eyes.

"We can't have this in Witherell," he said. "Got to restore law and order."

"There's no time for that just now," Reeves observed.

But Fogel was beyond listening to the facts. "I'll bring you in under my protection..."

Reeves was dumfounded. "You laying a charge agin me?"

"No charge." Fogel's eyes were glassy. "For your own good, is what I mean. Protective custody like. Until things settle down. Don't make a fuss about it now."

Fogel raised his pistol, languidly.

Something snapped in Reeves. He lunged forward and batted the gun out of the Sheriff's hand. Seizing the man by the lapels of his coat, Reeves shook him like a rag doll. "Your mealy-mouth line got my posseman killed, you spineless rat!"

He gave Fogel a last shake before slamming the man's head into one of the poles supporting the roof. There was the dull, wet smack of impact and Fogel slid to the floor to lay face down in the hay, unconscious.

Without a glance backwards, Reeves swung up into the saddle and kicked the horse into a gallop.

*"Your mealy-mouth line got my posseman killed, you spineless rat!"*

The Sinclair sawmill operated a half mile or so east of town. According to the map he and Rain Crow had studied on the ride in across the border, Sinclair owned most of the acreage surrounding Witherell and kept a big spread three miles from the mill. Reeves used the fading daylight to find the path angling up through the trees and brush. The winking of lanterns up ahead as he climbed showed him he was headed in the right direction. Despite the need for haste, he paused to study the path. The rain the night before had softened and molded the earth to a uniform smoothness. At several points he found the hawthorn branches broken, bent backwards, twisted beneath sand plum trees and bloodtwig until they resembled snakes and this seemed to satisfy him. He reached the mill as full dark descended.

The grind of the mill wheel and the splash of water it churned through covered his approach. He drew to within one hundred yards of the building before the whining tone of the saw blades inside lowered in pitch and the wheel creased to turn, the wooden buckets clacking wetly as they swayed.

Advancing cautiously, he used the trees for cover. The mill was at the base of a steep hill he remembered from the map though the area the hill occupied was rendered black by the lanterns lighting the mill. The first stars appeared and they began to haul the moon up into clear sky over the night hours like horses leading a stagecoach.

Reeves did not know if the sudden shutdown of the mill was due to what had taken place in town or was the normal end of the day's work. But he knew Sinclair would be there, preferring the proximity to town rather than the isolation of his homestead. He opted for the shotgun over his rifle as he knew he'd be outnumbered and slid the weapon from the scabbard on one side of the horse. The two cartridge belts he wore held rounds for the shotgun as well as ammunition for the Colts. He hobbled the horse on a grassy knoll bordered by screening trees and continued on foot.

Having lived with the Creek and Seminole for years in his youth, he'd picked up more than their language. The art of silently passing through the forest had also been shown to him and, being a runaway slave back then, he'd been a quick study. Silent as the grave, he inched closer to the mill.

The sight of the first gunman stopped him cold. The man leaned on the guard rail of the wooden footbridge next to the wheel gently nudged by the flow of water beneath it. It was clear to Reeves that at least one of the agitators in the crowd at Nelson's, probably Tim Hemp, had headed straight up to the mill to spread the word while the others had taken after him and Rain Crow.

The thought of his murdered posseman made Reeves grind his teeth together as he gripped the rifle in his huge hands. It had been a fine set up that had produced deadly results but Reeves was wise to the game now. All of his suspicions had been confirmed. The man he had hunted to Witherell had been murdered. There was a fresh target now.

Only this one was guarded. Time was on his side, however, so long as the conditions at the mill did not change.

Reeves stayed put for twenty minutes to let full night descend on the area and to let the one guard he could see, as well as any others, have their night vision reduced by boredom and the lanterns burning here and there.

When he felt he had waited long enough, he glided closer, making no sound. A patch of field stones had been laid near the mill to halt the encroaching forest now concealing his position. One portion of the stones lay in deep shadow. He carefully slid off his boots and wet socks, then started across the stones.

The shadows swallowed him up and he crouched, his back pressed to the wall of the mill, to let more minutes slip by.

Reeves was not idle during this time. He strained his ears trying to pick up any sound, a whisper, the scrape of a boot heel, the hissing draw on a smoke—anything that would allow him to clarify how many men lay in wait for him. Over the creak and groan of the wheel he thought he heard whispers overhead. Two of them were in an upper window. Reeves craned his neck up but the pointed roof of the mill and top window were lost in the night. A boot scraped not too far off but he could not tell from where it had come. That made four and Sinclair—if he was not part of the men Reeves had discovered.

He concluded that the only immediate threat was the man above him on the walkway. As this was also the only approach to the mill entrance on this side of the building, Reeves had to get past this man.

Turning his head this way and that, no avenue of approach presented itself, until he looked up at the end of the walkway directly above his head. Leaning gingerly to one side, Reeves saw that the walkway ended abruptly with a right angle turn just past the door and that there were no slats beneath the railing; just boards of stout hickory nailed to the support posts. More than enough space for him to fit through if he could make it.

He moved with the silent grace of a panther as he neared the lattice of beams. The crisscrossing wood was solid, meant to bear the weight of many men and equipment. The damp wood did not protest his weight as he began to climb with agonizing slowness. He had to keep one hand on the rifle, always aware of where the long barrel was placed before he moved lest the metal barrel or solid butt thump unexpectedly against the beams. There was a mindless rhythm to the movement of the buckets at the mercy of the flowing stream. Reeves timed his larger movements to these covering sounds and he rose up closer to the top. Like a spider he climbed and reached the edge of the walkway at last. The man had his back to him, peering into the night for Reeves to ride in from the opposite direction.

Reeves lay the rifle down on the walkway, freeing both hands to lever himself up. He got his elbows braced, then walked up the angle of the top beam until he could hook his knee around the railing post. From this position he heaved his body onto the walkway. This was the most dangerous part of the climb. The thick beams below consisted of wood soaked daily in the spray off the water wheel. Not so the thinner planks on top. A rusted nail, a board warped by the sun could produce a creak or groan at any second to give him away and this was no time for noise.

Using every bit of experience in the mastering of Indian ways, he slid up onto the platform, got his feet under him and rose to a standing position. If not for the continuous noise from the wheel, he was not sure he could have pulled it off. Luckily the man was standing right next to the wheel, the noise more than ample to cover the sound of Reeves moving fifteen feet behind him.

Reeves left the rifle where it was and drew one pistol. He gripped it around the cylinder, then closed stealthily in on the man who leaned on the rail, his rifle propped on a post near his leg as he finished a smoke. Up on the balls of his feet, Reeves placed each step with painstaking care.

Finally he was within arm's reach and swung the pistol like a club viciously against the back of the man's head, crushing his skull. Reeves lunged forward to catch the lifeless body before it collapsed. He wrapped his huge arms around the dead man and lowered the body to the walkway. He took up the feet to prevent any last autonomic tremors in the legs from scraping the worn hobnail boots along the wood. In a few moments all motion ceased and Reeves stretched the legs out.

Mindful of the need for silence, he returned to his shotgun, snatched it up, eased open the door and stepped into the mill.

It was his eyes that needed to adjust now as he was inside on the mill floor lit by many lanterns. There was a water barrel just inside the door and Reeves used it for cover, then peered around it to take in his surroundings. The circle saw gleamed, lethal in its stillness. The flat track propped several inches off the ground ran alongside the length of the mill floor. Saw dust covered every inch of the room, formed small cones in every corner and the air carried a host of smells from pine to cedar and rosewood.

With his eye on the windows, Reeves moved deeper into the mill, using the machinery for cover. Stepping over the flat track, the small offices were directly ahead. A lantern lay cold on a shelf outside the biggest office but it wasn't time for a light. Shotgun ready, he eased back the partially open door and pounced.

The room was unoccupied.

Dammit! He'd guessed and guessed wrong. Sinclair was not in his office. The plan had been for Reeves to collar his man inside the plant, cold cock him to keep him quiet, then carry him out via the cleared walkway and back to his horse for a ride out to the Lemon place and the waiting prisoner wagon. That was up in smoke now. And time was against him. How long before someone went to check on the walkway man? Then there'd be hell to pay.

Only he wasn't leaving without Sinclair. Reeves had to hope all his planning wasn't for naught. He had to give Sinclair credit. The man was out on the front line, not cowering in his office while his boys did his dirty work. This was not going to stop Reeves from dragging the man back to Fort Smith however.

He searched the other offices as a matter of course. They were deserted as well. In the process he spotted another of Sinclair's men. The man had his back to a window, a rifle over one shoulder as he stared out into the silent black from the log deck on the side of the mill facing the mountain. The air vent in the last office brought the earlier whisperers closer. He followed the line of the ceiling with his eyes, then exited. There was a staircase at the end of the corridor.

Reeves risked climbing the stairs as one of the whisperers sounded familiar and he dared to hope. He stopped at the landing to a storage loft shrouded in darkness. To one side was a narrow office. Reeves could not be sure of the identity of the whisperers as only faint moonlight leaked in through a small window in the office and he could not see them but he heard them well enough from the top of the stairs.

"Climb off, Sinclair!" hissed one of the voices. "I'm not to blame for Bennett's failing. We held up our end."

"Then why are we here in wait for that damned Marshal? You answer me that!"

Reeves recognized Sinclair's voice. The other had to belong to Tim Hemp. He didn't need to hear anymore. He retraced his steps.

"Charlie's been laid out!" cried a voice outside. "Reeves is here!"

The Marshal was halfway down the stairs when the shout came. He heard Sinclair and Hemp voice their surprise and feet pounded overhead.

There was nothing for it now.

Passing by Sinclair's office, he saw the gunman from earlier. He was half turned, uncertain, as he listened to the shouts of his fellows. Reeves raised the rifle and shot the man through the side. The man cried out and fell.

"Where'd that come from?" Voices rang out all around. "Anyone hit?"

Reeves was on the shop floor. He rushed to the control panel and got the wheel and saws going. The shrill whine was deafening.

A shot shattered a glass dial panel to his right. Reeves ducked and returned fire at the crouched figure at the window. He missed.

"He's on the floor!" the man outside the window yelled, keeping out of sight. "We got him trapped!"

Reeves fired again, shattering the glass in the window. He fired at all the windows he could see and the tinkling of falling glass was lost in the roar of the blades.

He hunched in a dark corner to consider his next move. He couldn't leave without Sinclair. He owed Rain Crow that much. But he also couldn't stay in the mill forever while surrounded by gunmen slowly closing in for the kill.

Feet pounded, men were yelling, a stray shot at some fleeing shadow split the night and was followed by another in quick succession.

The hand had been dealt and it was time for Reeves to go all in.

He crossed the mill floor quickly, snatching up a lantern on the way. A quick shake assured him there was oil in the lamp. Reeves stopped at the open sawdust barrels in a row just outside the rear door. The matches in the oilskin had survived the dunk in the stream and with sure movements he got the lamp going. The flame weaving like a cobra, he tossed it into a barrel midway along the line. At first the sawdust, damp from the rain, only smoked but it caught soon enough. Reeves didn't wait around to see them all go up.

The fire would bring all of Sinclair's men close to the mill and Sinclair out into the open as the building would go up like kindling. He knew their natural inclination would be to assess the fire and they'd lose their night vision in the process. Reeves did not wait around to be cornered when one of them stumbled upon him. Using the roar of the fire to cover his movements, he bolted from the heat building inside the mill and out into the chill of the night air.

The covering noise worked both ways and he did not see the gunman suddenly rearing out of the dark until the man was almost on top of him. Reeves got the shotgun up and fired, catching the man in the chest. The man reeled back, his finger tightening on the trigger of the revolver he held and the sound of another shot banged through the night to join the echo of the shotgun blast through the trees.

"Back this way!" a voice roared. "The log deck, I think!"

The disembodied voice had been correct. Reeves was halfway to the angled wooden deck with massive logs balanced on the sloping ramp leading down to the circle saw. Arcing, dancing tongues of flame devoured the plentiful supply of wood and lit the log deck like it was high noon. Approaching shadows moved in the flames. Sinclair and his men were closing in. Time was the deciding factor now.

Shots came his way, chipping the wooden beams of the deck to his left. These were followed by shots from the other side of the deck, spurred by the first volley and went wild.

The shots had missed him but had struck dead center into his plan to hide beneath the massive logs and use the brightness of the fire to allow him to slink into the deeper shadows around the blaze. Now they were closing in from both sides of the deck.

"We've got him now, boys!" shouted Sinclair, triumphantly. "Only don't kill him! I've got to find out what he knows first!"

That last part gave Reeves something to think about. He fired the shotgun at a moving shadow, heard a grunt of pain as someone took a stray pellet or two. The gun was empty and there was no time to reload. He dropped it and drew his pistols.

Bullets whizzed by and Reeves stooped for the cover of the log deck. The beams and the wood overhead blocked out most of the firelight and he moved blind at first through spider webs and stumbling over tongues of bark that had dropped from above to carpet the ground. The shots continued to come his way but they smacked into the thick beams or screamed off the iron collars around the wood.

The firing stopped and he heard hushed voices and the scuffle of boots. They were looking for him, following Sinclair's orders to take him alive. Good. That meant he still had a chance. His plan was a simple one but not without its dangers. At the far end, the log deck towered over his head. But it angled down to just a foot or two off the ground at the opening into the mill so the logs could be rolled down inside as needed. The doorframe was burning fiercely and he'd have to jump for all he was worth. Still if he could get to the lower end of the deck, he might catch them by surprise with a sudden leap through the fire. Once in the mill, he knew the door leading to the front walkway was unguarded. From there, the dark woods would be his destination and they wouldn't find him there as he kept track on Sinclair's movements and thought out a new plan to get the irons on the man.

He heard the voice getting closer. Saw shuffling feet at the far end of the deck.

It would have to be now.

Reeves fired off two quick shots to get their heads down and sprang into action. Crouching he was at the lowest point he could reach in seconds. He leaped out from the cover of the deck, then bounded up onto the smoldering log locked in place just outside the burning door frame. Balanced like a cat, he prepared to jump through the fire.

"Don't you move, you old son of a bitch!" The hissed warning was followed up by the click of a rifle being cocked.

Reeves got his hands up, turning slowly as sweat streamed down his face.

Tim Hemp had a rifle aimed right at his heart. Brown face gleaming with sweat, Hemp looked like he was ablaze himself as his red shirt caught the firelight while his black trousers turned his legs invisible against the light from the dancing flames.

"Got him, Sinclair!" Hemp yelled over one shoulder.

The men quickly gathered around Reeves, relief evident in their worn expressions as they kept him covered with their pistols.

Sinclair came around one side of the log deck, a rifle in his hands. He was sweaty, sooty, his clothes blackened yet he presented an air of someone who could not be diminished by these indignities to his person. The expression on his face was one of pure hatred his genteel words could not conceal.

"You have caused me a serious setback, Marshal," he said as he came to stand before Reeves. Hemp standing behind Reeves held up the two Colts so Sinclair could see their quarry had been disarmed. "Men get him away from the damned fire. We're burning up!"

Hemp shoved Reeves hard between the shoulder blades. Sinclair retreated until they were a safe distance from the blaze. Hemp and two other men went to join their boss and stood facing Reeves who had his back to the fire. A step in any direction and Sinclair's men would cut him down.

Sinclair regarded Reeves for a moment. "I should kill you for what you've done here. The mill is a ruin. I have men dead. However your acumen demands I have some answers first."

"What do you want to know about first? Why you murdered Running Elk? Why you murdered Jim Hill? Or why you murdered your wife? Take your pick."

Sinclair took a step back at this last revelation, then regained his composure. "The beginning, please. How in the world did you learn about my wife?"

Reeves crossed his big arms and glared at Sinclair. "Because Fogel's a damn fool who don't know when to shut up. Told me how you suffered the woes of Job getting your wife out here—not long after the Doc had left, I expect. Funny it wasn't so urgent while he was around those years. Urgent now, though, because a new Doc'll arrive sooner or later. So you got her here and murdered her in her bed. What was it? A pillow? Poison? My money is on the pillow, no evidence for a careful man such as yourself."

Sinclair's eyebrows rose on his forehead. "You do live up to your reputation," he said.

"Only Running Elk saw you do it, didn't he?" continued Reeves. "Word was there'd been robbing all over Witherell. Well that's natural for a lawless town. Only no one could catch Running Elk at it. Then your turn came. That lonely spread of yours ran more to the taste of Running Elk than the town jobs. 'Cept he came away with more than he'd bargained for, didn't he? He was a cunning thief and no fool. He knew what he'd stumbled onto. "

"You astonish me!" said Sinclair with genuine emotion. "However did you figure that out?"

"You were the only one in town certain Running Elk was the cause of all the town's problems. Said you'd stake your reputation on it if I recall. But it was something else got me thinking along those lines."

"Enlighten me. I am enthralled."

"The gunbelt Running Elk wore the night he was murdered. Expensive, finely tooled only not worn down by time. If Running Elk had stolen it off someone passing through, it'd had the marks of hard trail use upon it. But it didn't show much in the way of long use—like it had been sitting idle a good while. And you couldn't shoot since the accident years ago, could you?"

Sinclair slapped a hand down on one knee. "Well done, Marshal. You are right of course. That damned Indian put his hooks in me after I sent that shrew of a wife to her reward. He demanded the belt and I gave it to him. It was of no use to me and no one in town had ever seen me wear it. He wanted money and I gave him that, too."

"You didn't like that. Comes along Jim Hill, fresh out of hell on the border.

"Yes! I met him accidently in an Arkansas cat house. He was most receptive to my offer."

"I don't doubt it. He rode by easy pickings on the way to town because there was a Christmas turkey waiting on him in Witherell."

"He shot Running Elk right here at the mill," said Sinclair, nodding. "I set it up and Hill pulled the trigger."

"Then you had Hill drag the body down the trail into town, the scrub up here is full of Hawthorn and still bears the damage if you've got an eye to spot it, to make it look like Hill caught Running Elk out in the open. Put his body, all cut up from thorns, on display so everyone could celebrate with you. Your wife was dead, you had her Jennings money and the only witness was the town thief killed by Hill out of the goodness of his charitable heart."

"Then you came along, asking questions, sticking your nose in." Sinclair's expression darkened and he glared at Reeves.

"Killing Hill and pinning it on me and Rain Crow was your mistake. Because you left it in the hands of Bennett and Hemp, two fools who couldn't find their backsides with both hands."

Hemp didn't like that and raised his rifle. "Watch it, old timer."

"Mr. Hemp here is a crude lout," began Sinclair. "However I do have to echo his sentiments. Marshal Reeves you have impressed me. You have carried out your duty to the end and your work has been nothing short of extraordinary. I am truly sorry for what must follow but there's simply no other choice. Is there anything you wish to add?"

Reeves nodded, then tilted his head up and gazed at the stars. "You gents heard enough?"

An arrow thudded into the chest of Hemp, appearing suddenly as if by magic. The instant pain made him fire off a shot into the dirt as he staggered from the impact. Three shots rang in quick succession. They struck the gunman at Sinclair's left and as he fell, a second arrow lanced into the throat of the gunman behind him.

Hemp was on one knee, struggling to raise his rifle. Reeves lunged for one of his dropped guns and fired. The first shot caught Hemp in the chest, the second through one cheekbone. Hemp collapsed onto his back in the dust.

From the trees to one side of Reeves appeared Moz and Brown Bear. Brown Bear thrust his revolver into the pouch at his waist, clapped Reeves on the shoulder, then went to examine the dead men. Moz, an arrow notched in his bow, one eye locked on Sinclair, went to stand with Reeves. Switching his bow to one hand, he lit his cold stogie.

"You in one piece, Bass?" he asked.

"Right as rain," Reeves replied. "You cut it mighty fine. What took you so long?"

"Come by town on the way in, you said back in the clearing. That's what we done. Did the runaround with that no account Sheriff before we hit on the mill. You made enough noise up here to confirm our thinking and the fire lit the way and we got here while you and them others was shooting up all of creation. We lent a hand when it was needed just like you asked. What you complaining about?"

Sinclair had recovered his voice. "You amaze me, Marshal. Truly. Very well, I am a man who can roll with what life throws at me. I had an arrangement with Hill, I'll gladly make an arrangement with you. How do we settle the matter between us? Name your terms."

Reeves strode up to Sinclair, clutched him by his cravat and pulled him close so that their faces were inches apart.

"You'll stand before Judge Parker, then you'll swing for killing your wife, Jim Hill and Rain Crow." He thrust the man backwards with such force that Sinclair sprawled in the dust. "You can make all the arrangements you want with the Devil himself after that."

THE END

# A True Legend

Receiving the invitation to contribute a tale to this anthology was one of those pleasant surprises one encounters from time to time in the publishing biz. It's only been a couple of years since I heard the name Bass Reeves but I was immediately taken with the history of this incredible individual and, of course, began thinking of ways I could explore the real life character in a fictional context.

Having never written a Western before, I did not know what shape such a work would take but it was always on the back burner. So when our intrepid editor, Ron Fortier, dropped an email into my inbox stating Airship 27's intentions to put together a Bass Reeves book, I was hooked. When he went on to tell me who else had signed on to the project, I thought I'd died and gone to heaven. What great company!

My excitement was tempered by a bit of fingernail chewing because the other contributors were no slouches and I was certain they would turn in tales that were absolutely top notch. Yeah, I had to bring my A-game if I was going to stay with this posse. Well, you've read the results and I hope you've enjoyed my offering.

Before you move on to the next tale in the book, here are some of the behind-the-scenes details about my tale. Hopefully, these will give you a chance to catch your breath before saddling up for the next ride.

As always for me, the historical research is the first order of business. Relatively speaking, there's not much on Bass Reeves beyond the essentials of who he was and what he did and I was able to get a sense of the man from what has survived. Delving into the history of the Indian Territory was fascinating as I knew very little about it going in. What a rich landscape to set a tale. It had everything both good and bad and creating a cast of characters of heroes and villains was as easy as it was fun with so much elaborate history to choose from. Most of that history is unpleasant but the past is the past. It can't be changed and should never be sugar-coated.

As the territory was wild and mysterious, unmanageable with what amounted to a handful of Deputy-Marshals, I chose to bring the reader in slowly, gradually before springing the full unlawfulness of the area to explode in the reader's face. After that, it was all about Bass and Rain Crow in a hostile land, trying to do their jobs and stay alive in the process. How does a Marshal enforce justice when every hand is against him? When his presence is shunned instead of welcomed? If you're Bass Reeves, you use your head, rely on wits and intimidation and keep working the case. A six shooter can only do so much against an entire town.

I also wanted the case to be an intricate one. Westerns have been around a long, long time and there have been thousands of books, stories, TV shows, movies, serials, radio shows, comics—the list is endless—so, really, there's nothing truly original under the Western sun anymore. But that doesn't mean a writer should simply fall back on the tried and true clichés. The real Bass Reeves and today's reader deserve better. Thus I tried to be innovative with some of the Western tropes and I hope I've succeeded.

Bass Reeves is one of the great historical figures of all time. It's tragic his story is only now rising to prominence but, ultimately, gratifying that he is getting his due at last. We're going to be hearing a lot about Bass Reeves in the next few years and I hope folks will be listening to what is being said. Not only is he a tremendous figure from the past, but he is, and should be, an inspiration for people today. It was an honor and a privilege to add a few lines of fiction to the legacy of a man whose story needs no embellishment. Bass Reeves is a man for the ages.

ANDREW SALMON - Pulp Factory Award winner, Ellis and multiple Pulp Ark and Pulp Factory Awards nominee lives and writes in Vancouver, BC. His work has appeared in numerous magazines, including Pro Se Presents, Masked Gun Mystery, Storyteller, Parsec, TBT and Thirteen Stories.

He has published or appeared in:

*The Forty Club* (which Midwest Book Reviews calls "a good solid little tale you will definitely carry with you for the rest of your life"), *The Dark Land* ("a straight out science-fiction thriller that fires on all cylinders" - Pulp Fiction Reviews), *The Light Of Men*, which has been called ("a book of such immense significance that it is not only meant to be read, but also to be experienced... a work of grim power"—C. Saunders), *Secret Agent X: Volume One* and *Three, Ghost Squad: Rise of the Black Legion* (with Ron Fortier), *Jim Anthony Super Detective Volume One, Sherlock Holmes Consulting Detective Volumes One—Five, Black Bat Mystery Volume One, Mars McCoy Space Ranger Volume One, Mystery Men (&Women) Volume Two, Moon Man Vol. One, The Ruby Files Vol. One, The New Adventures of Thunder Jim Wade Vol. One, The New Adventures of Major Lacy Vol. One, The New Adventures of Lynn Lash Vol. One Ghost Boy Vol. One, All-Star Pulp Comics #2, Fight Card Sherlock Holmes: Work Capitol* and *Fight Card Sherlock Holmes: Blood to the Bone*

To learn more about his work check out:

amazon.com/Andrew-Salmon/e/B002NS5KR0/ref=sr_ntt_srch_lnk_7?qid=1328666769&sr=1-7

lulu.com/AndrewSalmon and lulu.com/thousand-faces.

# A TOWN NAMED AFFLICTION

By Derrick Ferguson

"Somebody comin', paw."

Bass Reeves twisted around, maintaining his balance on the top rail of the corral. His youngest boy, Edgar pointed up the wide, well-worn trail that was the main route to and from the Reeves ranch. Bass narrowed his eyes slightly as he looked at the distant rider. Behind him he heard the grunting curses of his oldest son Robert struggling with breaking the Spanish Mustang he'd been fighting with since early that morning. It was now mid-afternoon and neither horse nor man showed any sign of giving up or giving in.

"Looks like two riders, paw," Edgar said. Bass nodded. If his eyes stayed as sharp as they were now, Edgar would be an excellent hunter and tracker one day. There were indeed two riders but the one in the rear sat slumped over his saddle as if injured.

"Go on in the house and tell your ma to get the table ready. Looks like one of 'em is hurt. Then fetch me my rifle."

Edgar took off like a rabbit, kicking up a dust trail as he did so. Bass twisted around so that he would drop to the ground on the outside of the corral. Robert hadn't noticed a thing. He was still too busy with his Spanish Mustang. Bud and Colly saw the riders coming and they also got down from their perches on the top rail and came to stand slightly behind Bass. The riders came closer and Bass could indeed see that the second rider was hurt. Even from this distance Bass could make out blood on his shirt.

"Bass," Colly said in the high, quavering voice of his that always made him sound nervous even when he wasn't. "One of 'em got blood on his shirt."

"I see. Just stay where you are. Let 'em come to us."

"Both of 'em white men," Bud said around his generous chaw of tobacco.

"You figger them fer outlaws, Bass?" Since the only white men Bud mostly had ever had any dealings with were either lawmen or outlaws, he tended to think that any new white men he saw fell into one of those two categories.

"Naw. They ain't outlaws. At least the one in front ain't. He's law." Now that he was closer Bass suddenly realized that he knew the man.

Edgar pressed against his side, holding up his rifle. Bass patted the boy on the shoulder. "Give that to Colly. Colly, you keep your eye on the road, hear? You see anybody, sing out but don't shoot less'n they shoot first or I tell you to."

Colly took the Winchester from Edgar and held it in the crook of his arm, fixing his eye firmly on the road.

The two horses and their riders had come close enough that Bass could indeed identify the first man. He was also bleeding but the blood hadn't stood out due to him wearing a dark colored shirt. Bass went forward, motioning for Bud to go get the other man. Bass grabbed the reins of the lead horse, brought him to a stop. "Whoa there, whoa boy."

The man on the horse grinned at Bass. It was a grin full of ghastly humor. "Goddamn if'n it didn't take me a long time to get to your place, Bass Reeves." The man slid off his saddle, unconscious. Bass caught him, eased him to the ground.

"This 'un is dead, Bass." Bud said.

"Help me get this one into the house," Bass ordered. "Colly, you stay out here and keep watch. Edgar, go on 'round to the south road and keep your eyes on it. Anybody comes from that way you tell Colly." Bass grabbed the battered, bleeding man under his arms while Bud took his legs and the two of them carried him to the main house of the Reeves ranch. The door of the kitchen opened. A remarkably attractive young girl stood there, eyes open wide in surprise and fear. "What is it, Pa? Are we being attacked?"

"No, Sally. Close that door." Bass and Bud placed the injured man on the long kitchen table. Normally used for the preparation of meals it did double duty as an operating table when necessary. Nellie Jennie Reeves already had pots of water boiling on the stove. Sally, the oldest Reeves daughter had fetched plenty of clean cloths and the satchel of surgical tools. While no licensed physician, Nellie had done more than her share of doctoring on shot up men, including her husband. She tied up her long torrent of black hair into a bun on top of her head and looked at her husband. Bass had an odd expression on his face that she read accurately.

"You know this man."

Bass nodded. "Deputy Marshal Corky Burress. I rode posseman for him two, three times. He's a good man. A good marshal."

Nellie tied an apron around her waist. "He a friend of yours?"

Bass smiled slightly. "I wouldn't go so far as to say we shared the same bedroll but we've pulled a cork or two together. You think you can keep him alive?"

"Won't know until I get that shirt off him and see how bad he's shot up."

"You go on and get started. Bud, you stay here until I get back."

Bass left the kitchen and walked back to the corral, bellowing, "Robert! Quit foolin' around with that nag and come here! I got something for you to do!"

Robert Reeves looked up in consternation. "What?" Thus distracted, he wasn't able to compensate for the twisting buck the Spanish Mustang threw him. Robert went sailing through the air to land heavily on his back in a miniature storm cloud of dust. The Spanish Mustang trotted away and Bass could have sworn that the whinny the horse let loose with sounded suspiciously like triumphant laughter.

Robert painfully got to his feet and walked over to his father, brushing dust from his shirt and jeans. "Dammit, Pa! I almost had her. Just a couple more minutes…" he caught sight of Colly over his father's shoulder, still standing and watching the main road with the Winchester. And the dead man on the ground. "What's Colly doin'? Who's that on the ground? What's happenin'?"

"Deputy Marshal I know rode in all shot up with another man. That man's dead but your ma is workin' on the Marshal. I need you to get cleaned up and ride on into Fort Smith. You speak to Judge Parker and nobody else but Judge Parker, you hear me, boy?"

"Yessir."

"You tell Judge Parker that Deputy Marshal Corky Buress got himself all shot up and he's here at our spread. Tell Judge Parker I need him to advise me as to what I should do. If I should keep Buress here or bring him in."

"What about that other man?"

"You're going to help me carry him into the barn. More than likely he's Burress' posseman or cook. He can't be no prisoner 'cause he don't have no shackles on his wrists or ankles. I'll search him once we get him inside. He's sure to have papers or such on him. You doing okay there, Colly?"

"Sure, Bass."

By now, Bass was sure that nobody had followed Burress but it wouldn't hurt for Colly to stay on watch a few minutes longer. Bass and Robert picked up the dead man and carried him into the barn to deposit him in an empty stall. Bass hunkered down to quickly yet expertly search the man. "Nothing." He stood up, brushing his hands together. "If he was workin' with Burress he should have some paper on him. He'd need it to identify himself to law if he got separated from Burress or needed to operate on his own." Bass stroked his meticulously trimmed brush mustache with thumb and forefinger, a habit he indulged when deep in thought.

"You want me to mention this man to Judge Parker, Pa?"

Bass slowly shook his head. "I don't think so. I'd best find out from Burress who he is and what he was doing with him before complicating the issue. Just tell Judge Parker 'zackly what I told you to say. No more, no less."

"Yessir."

"And mind you come straight on back home with his word. You stay outta Miss Zenobia's."

"Pa…"

"Mind me, boy. This is business. Be off with you."

Robert headed toward the house to wash up and change his clothes. His father didn't expect him to dress in his Sunday clothes but to go see Judge Parker he did expect him to be neat and clean. Bass walked toward the house. "Colly! I think we're okay. You can leave off watching the road. Go tell Edgar the same."

Colly waved in confirmation. He and Bud were good men to have around the ranch. They worked for Bass when he needed some extra work done. Bass had acquired a dozen new horses last week and needed help in breaking them. Both Colly and Bud were expert horsemen and they worked well with Robert.

Bass went back into the kitchen, taking off his hat and wiping his forehead free of sweat. Burress lay on the kitchen table. Nellie had cut his shirt and jacket off him and cleaned his wounds. He'd been shot three times. Nellie had already removed one bullet from his shoulder. Bud stood nearby, ready to assist. Sally stood at Burress' head. A white cloth covered his mouth and nose. Sally held a bottle of ether at the ready. If it looked like Burress would regain consciousness, Sally would then let a couple of drops of ether drip onto the cloth. That would be sufficient to slip him back into unconsciousness.

"I sent Robert to Fort Smith to tell Judge Parker Corky Burress is here. We should know more 'bout what's going on by nightfall."

Nellie nodded, focused on her task. "You told that boy to stay out of Miss Zenobia's?"

"I surely did."

Nellie grunted in satisfaction, continued working. "You might as well go on and tend to your work. Bud can stay and help. I should be finished with him in an hour or so."

"He gonna live?"

Nellie nodded. "Lost a lot of blood but no vitals were hit, praise God. He'll be off his feet for a while but he'll live."

Bass nodded and left his wife to her work.

Bass knocked on the door of the guest room and upon hearing "C'mon in, Bass," turned the knob and went on in as bid. Corky Burress sat up in the huge four poster bed, propped up with four big goose down pillows. He was still pale as milk but his voice and his smile were strong. "Your missus said she'd send you up. How you be, Bass?"

"The more important question is how you be? And how you come to find yourself in such a predicament?" Bass held up a bottle of whiskey and two shot glasses. "This stays between us. If Nellie found out I was giving you liquor before she says so she'd beat me with a broom handle. She takes her doctorin' serious."

"She the one what patched me up?" Burress gestured at his bandages. "Damn good job she did. I'm obliged." He took the glass Bass offered and threw back the amber liquid in one gulp. Burress closed his eyes and shivered all over in delicious glee. "Now that's the stuff a man needs to recover. How long I been here anyway?"

"You been out for three days."

"Three days! Lordy!"

"You lost a lot of blood. Nellie said the best thing you could do was sleep." Bass pulled up a chair and refilled Burress' glass and filled his own. They clinked and drank. Bass put the bottle down between his feet. "Now what the hell happened to you, Corky? And who was that man with you? Your posseman?"

"Naw. He dead?"

Bass nodded.

Burress shook his head sadly. "Damn shame. If it hadn't been for him I'd have never gotten out of Affliction. I owed him."

"What were you doin' in Affliction?"

Burress held out his glass for another shot but Bass shook his head in a negative. "You do some 'splainin' first and then you get another drink. What's going on in Affliction?"

"You heard of the Chance brothers, right?"

Bass nodded. "I heard 'bout them. They go from town to town, the wide open ones that got no law. They make a deal with the folks who are fed up with their town being shot up ev'ry night and get themselves hired as town sheriffs. Then they run out them what owns the saloons, gambling joints and whorehouses and take 'em over for themselves. They then proceed to squeeze as much money outta that town as they can, then pack up and move on to the next one."

"That's them. There are four of them. Joe Chance is the oldest. Bob and Claude Chance come after him. Then there's Ricky. He's the youngest. They got a sister as well. Greta. She usually comes in after they've taken over the town to run the whorehouses for them."

"They got warrants on them?"

Burress nodded. "The man that was with me. His name is…was Seth Baker. Seth got enough of the townspeople to stand up with him and write up complaints against the Chance brothers. He brought them to Fort Smith. Well, Judge Parker has been sweatin' for months for just such an excuse to shut down the Chances. Judge Parker swore out the warrants and I asked to serve 'em."

"You did? Why?"

"I know Joe Chance back when he was a legitimate lawman down in Texas. I figured that would be in my favor. Figured that I could talk to him, make him see the sense in honorin' the warrants and come on in to talk to Judge Parker, him and his brothers. I told him I'd speak on his behalf and maybe Judge Parker'd be satisfied if they left the territory and worked their mischief elsewhere."

"So what happened?"

"Joe played along with me until he found out about Seth Baker and the others. He wanted to know who had sworn out the complaints 'gainst him and his brothers. When he did, that's when the killing started. Me and Seth barely made it out." Burress shook his head. "Joe Chance ain't the man I knew when he worked with me down in Texas. I looked in his eyes when we were talkin' and it was like lookin' into the eyes of a dead man, I swear, Bass. Whatever soul Joe Chance had just ain't there no more. I dunno what happened to change him so but he ain't the man I knew."

"Sounds like he turned out to be a bad 'un. Risky of you to go in and try to talk to him."

"Say it was a lawman you knew like me. Or Petrie. Or George Cornplanter. Or Cogburn. Wouldn't you do the same?"

Bass had to nod in agreement. "I s'pose I would. I'd give you a chance to turn yourself in and try to make it right, at least." Bass filled their glasses again. "I sent my boy off the day you come in to take word to Judge Parker 'bout your condition. He sent word back."

"And?"

"Judge Parker said I was to take whatever action I saw fit."

"And what action are you going to take?"

"What action do you want me to take?"

Burress sat straight up, wincing at the pain from his wounds as he did so but his voice was strong as he said; "Dammit, Bass! Don't sit there playing games with me! You know full well why I done rode to you!"

"You want me to go to Affliction and serve them writs on the Chances."

Burress fell back on his pillows. "Now was that so hard?"

"Mebbe I just want you to say it."

"Bass, will you go and serve them writs on the Chances? You know that we can't let them get away with this. Word has spread all over the territory by now that the Chances shot up a Deputy Marshal."

"Worse than that. Story now is that they hung you and killed half a dozen of your possemen." Bass grinned. "Story keeps getting' better every time I hear it. In 'bout a week they'll have it that the Chances slaughtered a whole passel of deputies."

"You know how stories get all twisted, Bass. I ain't askin' you to do this for me. We need to keep our reputation. The Chances get away with this and every other owlhoot in the territory will start walking around with their chest puffed out."

Bass nodded. "I done sent for Sonny Calvera to come posseman for me. Tom Lucky's gonna drive the wagon and cook. They should be here later on today. I'll leave in the mornin'. I'm gonna need those warrants. We can go over 'em after you've rested some more and et."

"You're just gonna take one posseman? That's all?"

"How many d'you figure I should take?"

"At least half a dozen, man! The Chances are all damn good shots and they ain't got much of a qualm about killin' I can attest to that!"

"Say I do round up half a dozen of the best deputy marshals we know and go a'riding into Affliction and call the Chances out. They decide to swap shots with us instead. Then what do we got? A whole lotta dead marshals. Maybe some innocent folks as well caught in the crossfire. Besides, that's what they'll be lookin' for, a show of force. Best to ease on in kinda sneaky like and check out the lay of the land first. Then I'll best know what to do."

Burress still looked dubious but he nodded and said, "Just as you please, Bass. Do it the way you see fit. By the way, Seth has a sister in town name'a Elizabeth. She runs a boarding house there. If you can get to her, she'll help you. At least she'll put you in touch with those in Affliction who want to see the Chances run outta town. At least those who are still alive, that is."

Bass nodded and took the shot glass from Burress. "Hey! You ain't give me one more for the road?"

"I would if you were going on the road but you ain't. You're gonna get some sleep. We'll talk some more after you done had your supper."

Burress stuck out his hand. "I'm obliged, Bass. You saved my life and I ain't gonna forget it."

Bass took his hand and shook it firmly. "You save your thanks until I catch them Chances and throw them in jail."

Bass sat on the front porch smoking his pipe and slowly rocking back and forth in his chair. Another twenty minutes or so and the sun would be extinguished for another day. The evening was always pleasantly cool here and it was one of his delights to smoke his pipe after supper and enjoy that cool evening breeze.

The front door opened and Nellie came on out to the porch and sat in the rocker next to Bass. "You had enough to eat, Bass?"

"Sure did. You know how I love me some chicken an' dumplings."

"Thought maybe they weren't seasoned to your liking. You only had three helpings."

"Got things on my mind. Been sitting here studyin' on how I'm gonna deal with them Chances." Bass suddenly cocked his head to one side. The sounds of digging he had been listening to for the past hour stopped. Bass bellowed, "Ain't nobody told you to stop digging, boy!"

The sounds of digging resumed. Satisfied, Bass replaced his pipe in his mouth and resumed rocking.

"Bass, how long you going to keep that boy on punishment?"

"I'm leaving in the mornin' His punishment will be up then."

"You done had him digging and building a new outhouse since he got back."

"An' he lucky I gots to leave otherwise he'd be building new ones for the Taylors and the Randolphs down the road. I told that boy to stay outta Miss Zenobia's. Smelled the likker on his breath the minute he got down off his horse."

"Now, Bass Reeves, you know full well that you like to have a drink or two yourself at Miss Zenobia's when you go to Fort Smith."

"That ain't the point, Nellie. The boy is free to waste his time all he wants when it is his time. I sent him on my business and he was on my time. I told him just as plain as I'm speaking to you now that he was to stay outta Miss Zenobia's."

"Bass…"

"Nellie, not more'n a month ago you was getting' on me about not being more of a father to the boys. Now when I'm trying to do as you ask you want me to be lenient. You can't have it both ways."

Nellie sighed. It was a sigh that Bass knew quite well by now. It was her "I'm not going to nag you about this no more but you'll have to bend some on the very next thing I ask you to do" sigh.

"Chirren in bed?" Bass asked.

"Yes. You ought to be going to bed soon yourself. You got a long ride ahead of you tomorrow."

"You right about that." Bass and Nellie rocked together for a while, not talking. Just looking up at the darkening sky as the stars began to appear. "Robert!"

"Leave off that digging. Go on in, wash up and have your supper. Then straight to bed. Your momma left you a plate on the stove."

"Yes, sir. Thank you, momma."

"You're welcome, Robert. You sleep well."

"Pa?"

"Yes, boy?"

"Good luck."

"Thank you, boy. Think you can have that Spanish Mustang broke by the time I get back?"

"I do believe I can."

"See that you do."

Bass and Nellie heard the shovel hit the ground and then the crunching of Robert's boots. The side door to the mud room opened and closed.

"How long you reckon you'll be gone, Bass?"

Bass puffed on his pipe for a bit before answering. "Well, it's not as if I have to go lookin' for them Chances. I know where they is so finding them ain't the problem. The problem is gettin' them to surrender."

*"How long you reckon you'll be gone, Bass?"*

"They shot up that man Burress something terrible. Don't you be comin' back to me all shot up like that."

Bass laughed a rich, warm laugh of genuine humor. "I will certainly do my best, wife. I certainly will."

"Quit'cher grumbling, Tom. You know full well I speak Chickasaw so I know what you're saying"

"If'n you know what I'm sayin' then why is we still on this damned road?"

Bass didn't bother to answer. Tom Lucky knew why they were on this road. Bass intended to stick to the back trails on their way to Affliction. Bass was well known in the Indian Territory by reputation. Even those who had never seen him were familiar with who he was and what he looked like. If it were known that he was out and about, word would spread fast and reach the ears of the Chances. And he wanted to put that off for as long as possible.

Tom Lucky drove the wagon, pulled by a team of four horses. The wagon was a huge contraption that not only hauled the cage in which prisoners were kept but also contained supplies for Bass, Tom Lucky and Sonny Calvera.

Tom Lucky had been a lawman for ten years, a member of the Chickasaw Lighthorse. Boasting an enviable and spotless record, it had come as a total and complete surprise to all when Tom Lucky suddenly up and quit. Tom Lucky gave no reason for his sudden resignation from that day to this. Of course the usual rumors went around that he had a dream about his death or that outlaws threatened him with death if he continued to ride with The Lighthorse. Bass had never asked him why he quit. A man's reasons were his own. Tom still worked as a cook and wagon wrangler and always came when Bass called and that was more than enough for him.

Sonny Calvera was fairly new in the Indian Territory, only been there for five years. But he already had a solid reputation as a posseman and Bass had worked with him two or three times before. Sonny was still rough but he knew how to keep his mouth shut and listen when it counted and Bass valued that in the youngster. There were so many who thought that they could get by with a fast draw and a brash attitude.

"All I was sayin' is that we spend an extra two days on the road goin' this way!"

"You got somethin' back home that needs doin'? Or you worried that them three wives of yourn goin' to run off with younger and better lookin' men while you're on the trail?" Bass half turned in his saddle to grin at Tom, who waved a dismissive hand in his direction.

"How we going to play this, Bass?" Sonny wanted to know. With his long, straight black hair, graceful manner and wide, dark eyes, at first some of the other deputy marshals said that he was too pretty to be a lawman and unmercifully teased him. One day Sonny wearied of the teasing and knocked out three of Sam Breedcock's teeth with one punch. The teasing ceased that same day.

"I'm gonna go in first. In disguise. Poke around for a bit; see exactly what we're up against. I know that we're gonna have to separate them Chance brothers. I got me an idea on how to do that. We'll talk on that some more over supper. Meant to ask you somethin', Tom," Bass slowed up his huge white stallion, Cisco, to allow the wagon to catch up and he rode alongside so that he could speak to Tom comfortably. "You worked down in Texas same time Corky Buress did. You ever run into this Joe Chance?"

Tom Lucky shook his shaggy head. "Heard of 'im, though. Wasn't many who didn't. Tough as they come. Quicker than a rattler with his guns. One'a the very few I know of to turn down an offer to be a Texas Ranger. Most badmen that got the word Joe Chance was on their trail lit out of Texas and stayed out."

"That good, huh?"

Tom nodded gravely. "That good."

"What would make a lawman that good turn bad the way he done? I mean, using the law to cover up killing and stealing?"

Tom shrugged. "You know how things can get, spendin' years tracking down the meanest scum alive. That changes a man, no matter what. It can't help but change him. Sometimes he pulls back, finds another way to serve. Other times he just says the hell with it." Tom cocked an amused eye at Bass. "Ev'vybody ain't like you, Bass Reeves. They don't make being a lawman a holy callin'."

Bass snorted. "I don't do that. I just do my job the best way I know how, is all."

Tom Lucky chuckled. "Just as you say, Bass. Just as you say."

"How do I look?"

Tom Lucky and Sonny Calvera eyed Bass Reeves as he emerged from around the wagon. He'd taken off the ankle-length duster, black suit, fine white shirt and immaculate Palacio hat and changed into quite different garb. His jeans and jacket both looked grubby and greasy as if he wiped his hands on them after eating. The once white shirt was gray and dingy. The hat looked as if it had been gotten hold of by an angry mutt sometime in the recent past. A .45 Peacemaker in a battered holster completed the disguise. The Peacemaker looked as weathered and worn as the rest of the outfit Bass wore. Nothing like the gleaming Colt revolvers that were his favorite weapon of choice.

"I wouldn't let you come inside my house looking like that," Tom said. "You want something to eat 'fore you go?"

"I'll eat in town. Both of you clear on the plan, right?"

Both Tom and Sonny nodded. Bass walked over to a horse that looked as broken-down as he did. It wouldn't do for a Negro to come riding into town on a fine white stallion like Cisco. Some white man would be sure to take exception and shoot him off the animal. Bass swung up on the nag and clucked at him. "C'mon, git up there." He rode off at a trot, waving his hat in salute at Tom and Sonny who waved back. The two men settled down to wait with a deck of cards and a pot of coffee.

The sun had only been in the sky for two hours but it was already warming up the day considerably. Bass kept the nag to a gentle trot and pointed the horse's nose in the direction of Affliction. Presently, the town came into view.

Affliction had sprung up maybe ten years ago when word of silver being found in the region spread through the territory. Mention the possibility of gold or silver in these parts and it didn't take long for men and women from far and wide to converge on the spot, looking to make their fortune overnight. Turned out that there was no silver. It had all been a scheme by a pretty shrewd band of slicksters who were the only ones that made a fortune selling worthless deeds to equally worthless land that they had sworn on a stack of Bibles was filthy with silver. By the time they cleared out, they inhabitants of Affliction looked around and found out that they had a pretty good town going, fueled by that various outlaws and bandits passing through who liked to spend their money there. Bass had been there once years ago when he had been posseman to Deputy Marshal Cholly Puente. He hadn't been in disguise then but had no fear that he'd be recognized. Who bothered remembering what a black man looked like?

Bass rode into Affliction, looking around without looking around. He'd been doing this long enough that he knew how to pick up on details that would escape most folks. Affliction looked just like any number of towns here in the Territory. Just from initial impression one wouldn't think that the town had any sort of problem at all.

Bass looked for The Baker House, the boarding house run by Elizabeth Baker. The sooner he got in touch with her the sooner his investigation could start in earnest. He secured directions from the town blacksmith and soon located The Baker House, located roughly in the center of town. Bass tied up his horse in front and walked around to the back. He politely knocked on the rear door. A minute later it was opened by a petite, fresh faced colored girl who looked Bass up and down with obvious approval. "Well, sir! Now what can I do for you this fine morning?"

Bass took off his hat as he said, "I'd like a word with Miss Baker, if you please. I got a message for her from her brother."

The girl's eyes narrowed. "You know where her brother is? You spoke to him?"

"Please, Miss…my words are for Miss Baker's ears."

"Missy? What's going on? Why aren't you keeping an eye on…" Over Missy's shoulder Bass could see a blond woman who had just come into the kitchen.

Missy held the door open wider, indicated Bass with a nod of her head. "Man here says he's got a message from your brother, Miss Baker."

Elizabeth Baker covered the distance from the kitchen door to the back door in no time flat. "Where's Seth? Is he with you? Is he okay?"

Bass quickly stepped inside the kitchen and closed the door. "It would really be best if we could talk somewhere in private, Miss Baker. Please."

Bass had to give her credit. She didn't waste any more time with words, just indicated that Bass should follow her. He did so, back through the kitchen door and through a long corridor whose floor fairly shone from being freshly mopped that morning. Elizabeth opened a door; indicated Bass should come on in. The room was her office most likely. There was a roll top desk, two chairs and not much else. The room was for business, right enough.

Elizabeth locked the door and turned around, a derringer in her hand. Her sky blue eyes glittered with anger. "You asked to speak to me in private. Okay, we've got privacy. I'll give you just two minutes to explain who you are, how you know my brother and what your involvement with him is."

Bass slowly raised his hand shoulder length. "You don't need that, Miss Baker. I'm a friend. Deputy Marshal Bass Reeves."

Elizabeth's eyes flickered with recognition. "I've heard the name. Show me some proof of who you are. You must have a badge, identification papers..."

"I didn't carry any of that with me, Miss Baker. As you can plainly see by my garb and the way I came around to see you, I don't 'zackly want it known that I'm in town as of yet."

Elizabeth slightly lowered the weapon. "Can't say how I blame you. If Joe Chance and his brothers knew there was a Deputy Marshal in town they'd kill you sure. But you said you had a message from my brother! What is it?"

"Ma'am, I beg your pardon for telling a lie like that to get in to see you. But I figured that news like this should be given face to face and in private. Your brother's dead."

Elizabeth slumped up with her back against the door. The hand holding the derringer dropped to her side. "I can't say I didn't think he was. He was hit at least three or four times riding out of town."

"He and Corky Buress made it to my place. My missus was able to save Buress but your brother was dead when he arrived. Must have died on the trail. His body is at my place and when this business is over I'll be more than pleased to bring him here to you so that you can bury him as you please."

Elizabeth replaced the derringer in the small hidden pocket of her dress. She nodded absently and walked slowly over to her desk and seated herself in the swivel chair. She looked up at Bass. Her eyes were dry but her voice trembled with emotion as she said, "Thank you for doing what you could for Seth, Mr. Reeves."

"Ma'am, Corky Buress said that you would be able to put me in touch with them who want to see the Chances run outta town."

"There are few of them left alive. Joe Chance himself killed three of them. Some of the others left that same night. There's only two or three left and they might not to want help you. Can't say as how I blame them."

"I've got a plan in mind to separate the Chance brothers. I think it will work. Which way is the Sheriff's office?"

"Just go out the front door, cross the street and it'll be four doors down. But if you're looking for Joe Chance, he won't be there. He spends his days at the Black Horseshoe, drinking. You'll find him there."

"Good. He's the one I want to see. And if he's been drinking, so much the better."

"Don't let that fool you, Mr. Reeves. I swear, I've never seen a man that drinks all day like Joe Chance but doesn't get drunk. He starts at nine in the morning and at nine at night he's still just as sober as if he never started."

"I can handle Joe Chance. You just get ahold of them others and tell them I want to meet them here in three hours. Can you do that?"

Elizabeth nodded. "I'll have them here. You just watch yourself around Joe Chance. He's fast, he's mean and he's smart."

Bass smiled as he gestured for Elizabeth to unlock the door so that he could be about his business. "I'm not given to brag, Miss Baker, but there's folks that would pretty much say the same 'bout me. I think me and Mr. Chance will get along just fine."

Bass walked up to the batwing doors of The Black Horseshoe saloon and peered in, taking measure of the interior before entering. Tables for Faro, poker and shooting dice were over to the left. A small stage was on the right, the curtains drawn. Far too early in the day for the dancing girls to be kicking up their heels and doing the can-can. A number of round tables were scattered about and at one of these tables, a big man sat there with a bottle of whiskey at his elbow, playing solitaire.

There were five men standing at the bar, quietly talking, but upon hearing the squeaking of the batwing doors opening, they turned. Two of them dropped their hands to their guns. Bass lifted his own hands to show he wanted no trouble.

The bartender frowned. "Nigger saloon is at the end of town, boy."

"Don' wan' no trubble, sah. Just lookin' for Sheriff Chance. Got some news fo' him I'm sure he want to hear."

The bartender looked over at the big man playing solitaire. "You know this boy, Sheriff?"

Joe Chance raised his eyes from his solitaire game and sized up Bass with eyes as dead as rocks. "New in town, aint'cha?"

"Yassuh. Jus' rode in an hour ago. Got some news for yuh I'm sure yuh want to hear."

Chance waved a hand at the bartender. "I'll take care of this, Clint. Go on back to taking care of your customers. You. Come on over here."

Bass slowly walked over to the table, taking his measure of Joe Chance as he did so. A blocky man of size with big hands. A three day growth of stubble covered his cheeks and chin. His hair might have been blond once.

It now was more silvery white than anything else. And dead and soulless those eyes might have been they didn't miss a thing. Bass would have to watch himself with this one.

Chance poured himself a drink. He gestured at the bottle. "Want one?"

"Nossir. I do my drinkin' in the evenin'. I 'preciate your courtesy, though."

"I'm Sheriff Chance. What's this news you got for me?"

"I was riding along east of here, cuttin' 'cross territory to save time. On my way to Ruthie's Point to see my sister. Muh brother-in-law's feeling poorly an' they need help to work the place..."

"You're wasting my time." Chance threw back a shot of whiskey. While his eyes were still dead his voice more than communicated his feeling.

"Yassuh. Don' means to be wastin' yo' time," Bass replied. He wondered if maybe he wasn't putting on the dumb darkie act a little too strong. It was hard to read this man. Joe Chance seemed to be as emotionless as a brick wall.

"Anyway, I'm comin' through a dry wash east of town an' I found me a couple dead men."

And now Chance did show some emotion. He put down his shot glass and looked up at Bass with eyes that at last had something new in them: suspicious fear. "You telling me the truth, boy? You know I can lock you up for lying to a Sheriff?"

"Yassuh. But I'm not lying. I brung this as proof." Bass reached into a pocket and withdrew something that he placed on the wooden table next to Chance's glass.

It was Corky Buress' bloodstained badge.

Chance picked up the badge, turned it over in his big hands as he said to Bass; "Anybody else know about this?"

"Nossir. I wuz by myself."

"You told anybody else in town about this?"

"Nossir. Just got into town. Don't know anybody here."

"How long you figure them bodies were out there?"

"Two, three days at most, suh. Looks like coyotes been at them."

"Why'd you come here to tell me about this?"

"Well...ain't you the law, suh? Ain't you supposed to do somethin' 'bout it?"

Chance's lips pressed together in what might have been anger. He quickly poured himself a last shot, drank it and slammed the glass down. "Come with me."

Bass followed Chance out of the saloon and they crossed the wide main street, dodging men on horseback and rattling wagons and sleek, elegant buggies. They gained the other side and walked to the Sheriff's office. There was one man inhabiting the office, sitting behind one of two desks. Bearded, with fine straight brown hair and acorn colored eyes as quick and sharp as those of a fox. He eyed Bass with open suspicion while saying to Chance, "Somethin' up Joe?"

"Where's Claude and Ricky?" Chance countered.

"Taking a turn around the town. What's goin' on? Who's this?"

"You go find Claude and Ricky and bring them back here quick. I only want to have to tell the story once."

The man, who Bass realized had to be Bob Chance, said no more. He got his hat and left on the double.

Joe Chance gestured at a chair. "Sit yourself there. When my brothers get back you answer their questions if they ask you any. You got that?"

"Yassuh."

"You want something to eat? I can have something brought over while we're waiting."

"Breakfast sho' sounds good, suh."

Chance nodded and opened the door, yelled at a boy loafing across the street and ordered him to go over to Lainie's and come back with a plate of ham, scrambled eggs and fried potatoes. Chance closed the door and walked over to the desk, seated himself behind it. "Lainie's serves the best food in town but they don't serve your folk."

"I 'preciate your hospitality, suh."

Chance took off his hat, threw it on the desk. He looked around as if missing something. Probably his bottle. "You don't have to 'yassuh boss' me every time you open up your mouth. I got me a suspicion you ain't as dumb as you make out to be. You don't move like a field hand and when you come in here you stood where you could not only cover me and my brother if you had too, but the door as well."

Bass said nothing but inwardly he was cursing himself. He should have paid attention to his instincts about this man. Joe Chance was no fool.

"And I understand. Knew quite a few nigras who pretended to be dumb in front of white folks to get by. I understand getting by." Chance dry washed his face with his big right hand. "What's your name?"

"Bill Butterfield."

"Well, Bill. You done stepped into a nice big ol' pile here. But you talk straight and do what I tell you and you'll come out of this just fine. I may even put some gold in your pocket if what you say pans out."

At that moment there was a knock on the door and the boy Chance had sent for the breakfast came in with a napkin covered plate. Chance indicated that he should give it to Bass. He flipped the boy a coin and indicated he should leave. Bass sat down at the other desk and attacked his food.

"Coffee's on the stove behind you. If you're lucky, Claude made it before he left. Bob can't make a decent pot of coffee to save his soul."

Bass nodded and got up to help himself. Chance was right. It was damn good coffee. He was halfway through when the door opened again. Bob Chance entered with the other two Chance brothers, Claude and Ricky.

Claude looked more like Joe than the other two. Same blocky body, same big hands. But his eyes were bright and full of life, a creamy color that Bass suspected women found fascinating. Ricky Chance, despite being the youngest, was the tallest. He also was thinner than his three brothers. He wore his guns tied down. According to Buress, Ricky was the one that fancied himself the fastest draw of the Chance brothers. "But don't you believe it," Buress had told Bass. "Ricky's fast as hell, yeah. But Joe can put a bullet between your eyes, put his gun back in the holster and be halfway back to the saloon before your body hits the ground."

"Here they are," Bob said irritably, not taking his eyes off Bass. "You gonna tell us now just what the hell is wrong with you?"

Joe gestured at Bass. "Mr. Butterfield here says he come across two dead bodies in a dry wash east of here. Been there more'n a few days. He brought this as proof." Joe threw the bloodstained badge on the desk. Bob picked it up. His eyes flickered to Bass, back to the badge then back to Bass. "Bullshit," he said with utter certainty. "Me and Claude searched all over for Baker and Buress. We didn't find 'em."

"Did you check that dry wash?"

"Weren't any need to! Their trail went nowheres near that wash." Bob's hand dropped to his gun. "He's lying. I dunno why or what for. But he's lying."

"Now hold on, Bob." Claude said. He held the badge. His thumb rubbed at the bloodstains. "We didn't search as well as we could have, I'll say that. We just figured that Baker and Buress had been shot up enough that they would die out on the trail far enough away from Affliction that it wouldn't matter." He looked directly at Joe. "We coulda missed their bodies."

"Well, here's what you're gonna do now," Joe said. "You and Bob are gonna ride out right now and go where Mr. Butterfield tells you he found them bodies. If they're out there, you're gonna bury 'em right where they are so nobody else finds them."

*“Mr. Butterfield here says he come across two dead bodies.”*

"And if we don't?"

The sudden cocking of a Colt revolver captured Bass's attention. Joe Chance had his gun out and had it pointed right at his head. "In that case I'm gonna have to hang Mr. Butterfield for whatever charge I feel like. He'll be right in a cell waiting for you boys to come on back and tell me one way or another what I got to do. Ricky, go on over there and get his gun."

Ricky did so and stood back a ways, grinning.

"Now just get up real slow and easy and make your way back on over yonder to that there open cell."

Bass did as he was told and walked into the cell. The slamming of the cell door coincided with the creaking on the bunk as Bass dropped his weight on it. "You don't have no call to be lockin' me up, Sheriff. I ain't did nothin' wrong."

Joe Chance locked the cell door. "Didn't say you did. But I'll feel better knowing that you're right where I can lay my hands on you if needs be. Could be that you're lying about those bodies being out there."

"What reason I got for doin' that, suh?"

Joe shrugged. "Got no idea. Hey, if those bodies are where you say they are, you got nothing to worry about. You'll walk away from this with some money in your pocket. You got my word on that. And besides, something about you makes the inside of my head itch. I'll feel better with you in here." Joe left the cell room, closing the door and returning to the main office. Bass heard him speaking to Ricky.

"I'm going on back to The Black Horseshoe. You take a turn around the town. Look for any more strangers showing up."

"What about the nigra?"

"What about him? I done fed him and he's locked up tight. We can leave him alone. I want to know if there are any other strangers in town. You see anybody you don't know, you come get me."

Bass listened intently for the sound of the two pairs of boots leaving the office and the door being shut. Bass heard Joe locking the office door.

Bass took off his left boot and shook it. Two skeleton keys fell out. He replaced that boot and took off the right one and shook two more keys out of there. He picked up the keys and grinned at them. He stood up and walked to the cell door. He tried one key after another in the lock. The third one opened it.

Bass walked over to one of the windows facing the street and looked out. He could see Joe's broad back crossing the street. Ricky must be on the sidewalk, heading away from the sheriff's office. He hadn't expected

Joe to lock him up but he had been ready for that eventuality. He walked back to the cell door and closed it again. He returned to the office and looked through the desk drawers until he found his gun. Joe and Ricky would have something to think about when they returned and found him gone. Bass had no intention of being here when they got back. Because if things went according to plan, Claude and Bob wouldn't be coming back.

"You just had to open your big mouth and tell Joe that we didn't check out that dry wash, didn't you?" Bob Chance snarled at his brother, riding next to him. "Couldn't just have keep your big mouth shut and let me do the talkin' could you?"

"You know just as well as I do that Joe can always tell when we're lyin'. Best to just own up and tell him we didn't do our job right the first time." Claude shrugged. "Besides, it ain't gonna take us that long and it's worth the work to keep Joe off our backs."

"You notice he's been drinkin' more than usual?"

"You never mind about that. I ain't never seen Joe drunk and neither have you. He's just got a lot on his mind right now. That marshal he shot was a friend of his from Texas."

"You reckon we have to worry about more marshals coming in from Fort Smith?"

Claude shrugged. "I reckon that sooner or later they'll send somebody to look for him. Me, I'm just gonna say that we never seen him and leave it at that. I suspect Joe is gonna do the same. I advise that you adopt a similar attitude."

"Me and Greta figure that we ought to pull up and get out while we got the chance. Get out of the territory altogether."

Claude snorted in derision. "You and Greta always want to cut and run when things get a little warm. You just follow Joe's lead. He'll see us through just like he's always done."

Bob subsided. He'd been through this before many times with Claude and it was always the same. Claude followed right behind Joe close enough to be his shadow. If it was alright with Joe then it was fine with Claude. It had been that way ever since they were kids. Bob was more like Greta than he was his brothers. He understood Greta more than he understood his brothers, really. Greta was like him. They both looked out for themselves and saw no reason to stay around when things started to get just a little too hot. And gunning down a Deputy Marshal as well as half a dozen prominent town citizens definitely qualified as a situation that was red hot.

Far as Bob was concerned, it would be better for all of them if they abandoned Affliction and headed back to Texas where they had friends and family that would look out for them. And he knew that Greta would be right behind him. But Claude and Ricky…as long as Joe said stay, stay they would.

"There's the dry wash," Claude said, pointing. Bob reached for his canteen, took himself a nice long cool drink of water. So his head was tilted back and he was not looking at the dry wash. That's why when Claude's gun boomed, he dropped the canteen in shock. Because he hadn't seen what Claude had seen.

Two men poked their heads over the edge of the dry wash, Winchesters in hand. Claude fired again; fighting to keep his horse under control since having the gun go off so close to its right ear immediately threw it into a panic.

One of the men shouted; "We're duly sworn and deputized agents of a Deputy Marshal! Surrender or see your asses blown to hell!"

Claude's response was to fire again. Bob left his gun where it was and went for his own Winchester. If he and Claude were to have a chance, they'd need to be able to match the extra range the Winchesters of their assailants had.

Seeing that Bob was going for the Winchester, Tom Lucky took his time and put a bullet right in Bob Chance's left leg. Bob yowled as if scalded and yanked on the reins, painfully twisting his horse's neck. His horse, disoriented by the shooting and yelling, decided that he had had just about enough of this. He bucked and twisted, throwing Bob off his back and thus unencumbered, took off at a mad gallop back in the direction of town.

Bob got to his feet, drew his gun and fired at Tom and Sonny Calvera, cursing a blue streak.

"Goddammit, Bob, get down!" Claude bellowed. His gun spent, he threw it away and reached for his rifle.

Sonny shot Bob right in the stomach. Bob screamed and clutched at the wound with one hand, still firing with the other. Sonny shot him two more times, right in the chest. Bob stumbled backwards several steps, fell to his knees and toppled forward onto his face.

"Bob!" Claude yelled. "Goddammit, BOB!" he still fought with his horse, tried to turn it around so that he could head back to Affliction and caught a bullet in the shoulder. Claude tumbled backwards off his horse and landed hard.

Being younger and lighter on his feet, Sonny scrambled out of the dry wash and ran over to where Claude struggled to get up. Sonny jammed the muzzle of his rifle into Claude's neck. "You stop moving 'fore I blow your head clean off, savvy?"

"Go see to my brother!"

Tom Lucky knelt next to Bob Chance, lifted his head up by the hair and looked into the open eyes that stared at nothing. Tom let the head thump back into the dirt. "Your brother's gone onto a better world. Or, if the stories I've heard 'bout you boys be true, a much hotter one."

"You sons of bitches!"

"Blame yourselves," Sonny suggested. "Didn't you hear us identify ourselves as deputized agents of a Deputy Marshal?"

"Any damn fool out here can say that! You showed no badge, no papers of any kind!"

"Yeah, and you being a Sheriff and all, why is it that soon as you saw our heads pop up, you started shooting without identifyin' yourself?"

Claude said nothing, just clutched at his injured shoulder and looked at the body of his brother.

"Get up. We'll patch you up and get you in the wagon," Sonny ordered. "Then I'll show you the legal warrant we got for your arrest and your brothers."

"Mister, I don't know who you and that old bastard think you are, but if you're figgerin' on taking down Joe Chance then you just as well put that gun to your head and pull the trigger. 'cause when Joe finds out you've killed Bob he's gonna make it his mission to put you six feet under."

"Bullshit," Sonny said with conviction. "C'mon, get up."

Claude struggled to his feet and slouched in the direction of the dry wash. "Yeah, you may have got me and Bob but mister, you still got to deal with Joe. And don't forget that there's still Ricky as well. And both of 'em are faster than lightning."

"We'll worry about that when it happens. You got your own problems to concern yourself with."

Claude stopped as a sudden thought hit him. "That nigger! They one told us he saw them bodies out here! He's with you!"

"Easy to tell that you ain't the brains of the bunch if'n it took you this long to figure that out. Keep moving. I ain't gonna tell you again."

"I guess you figgered he was dumb enough to not reckon on getting killed first, I guess. Joe's got him locked up back in Affliction and soon as our horses get back to town without us, Joe's gonna kill him first thing."

Both Sonny and Tom burst out laughing at that and neither one of them would shine the sunlight of illumination on the sudden fog of confusion that now choked the brain of Claude Chance.

Elizabeth Baker opened the rear door of The Baker House. Bass Reeves slipped in quickly and she closed the door. "I figured that had to be you. What happened to you? Where have you been?"

"Locked up in jail." He gave her a short but comprehensive outline of his activities since he had left her.

Elizabeth nodded in understanding. "That's why Bob and Claude rode out of town as if the devil were after them. And Joe still thinks you're locked up in his jail?"

Bass nodded. "He went back to the saloon. Ricky's taking a turn around the town but he could return to the jail at any moment and that's when things are going to really start happening 'round here."

"You need to get out of town before Bob and Claude come back."

Bass chuckled. "Right now Bob and Claude are either locked up or sitting down to lunch in hell. I got a couple possemen waiting out there in the dry wash I sent them to. By now they should have gotten the drop on them two. Or killed 'em, one."

Elizabeth nodded in satisfaction. "Can't say that I feel much sympathy for them. What are you going to do now?"

"Did you get ahold of them others you told me about?"

"I sent my girl Missy with messages that they should meet me here. They haven't gotten here yet. In the meantime, you'd best hide out in my office until they come. You don't want to be seen by the wrong people."

"I sure don't, ma'am."

Elizabeth led the way to her office, unlocked the door and held it open for Bass to enter first. She stepped inside and closed the door behind her. "Please, make yourself comfortable. Can I get you coffee? Maybe something stronger?"

"Coffee'd be just fine, ma'am."

"I just want you to know that I appreciate everything you're doing for this town, Mr. Reeves. My brother gave his life to get rid of the Chances and it does my heart good to know that he didn't get himself killed for nothing."

"I wish he didn't have to get killed at all, Miss Baker. I feel bad whenever a civilian gets killed doin' the job that a Marshal should be doing. Corky Buress should have known better than to get a civilian involved."

Elizabeth smiled. "You didn't know my brother, Mr. Reeves. He didn't believe in sitting back and doing nothing when there was a wrong to be righted. It was Seth who organized the folks in town and got them to write up complaints about the Chances. He took them himself to Fort Smith."

"Sounds like he'd have made a fine lawman himself, ma'am. Why didn't he get the job of Sheriff here?"

Elizabeth's face hardened. "Too many of the leading citizens wanted a quick fix to the problem we had. There was a pretty bad bunch running this town before the Chances killed them and took over. Those citizens just wanted the problem gone and didn't care how. Well, once the Chances took over and started squeezing them for money they quickly found out that they'd traded the fire they knew for the frying pan they didn't." Despite the seriousness of the situation, Bass had to laugh.

Somebody knocked on the door of the office. Bass slowly stood up, his hand going to his gun. Elizabeth said, "Who is it?"

"It's Harvey Mitchum, Lizzy. I got Bean Slater and Dave Massey with me."

Elizabeth opened the door and let the three men in. As one, their eyes opened wide upon seeing Bass standing there with his hand on his gun. The leading man, who Bass took to be Harvey Mitchum said, "What's going on in here, Lizzy? This man…"

"This man is the reason I called you three here. This is Deputy Marshal Bass Reeves and he's come to help us get rid of the Chances."

"Bullshit," Mitchum said. "I heard a' Bass Reeves. Supposed to be a sharp dresser. This nigra look like he stole them clothes from a beggar."

"Now, just hold on, Harv." The second man shoved forward. He took off his bifocals and with squinty eyes gave Bass Reeves a good looking over. He then nodded in satisfaction, replacing his bifocals on his face. "Yep. This here's Bass Reeves. I get 'round to Fort Smith two or three times a month. I've seen Reeves there a couple times. Warn't dressed like this, that's for sure but this is him." The second man stuck out his hand "Bean Slater, Bass. Pleased to meetcha." Bean made the introductions. "This here is Harvey Mitchum, runs The Smiling Girl, our leading gambling and entertainment emporium. Dave Massey owns the largest dry goods store in town."

"What's your line of business, sir?"

Bean smiled, showing an amazingly well-kept and bright set of teeth. "I'm the town undertaker."

"If you're really Deputy Marshal Reeves then where's your posse?" Mitchum demanded. "You're going to need at least a dozen men to take down the Chances."

"It's me and two other men. They're good men and by now they should have Claude and Bob Chance locked up. Or dead. All depended on what way they wanted it."

Mitchum still looked skeptical. "I'm not rightly sure what you want from us."

"Just this; I don't expect you to do my job. And this job has to be done by a Deputy Marshal. So I'm going to come back into town and have it out with Joe and Ricky my own self. All I need for you to do is quietly spread the word and get the people off the streets. I don't need to be worryin' about civilians. There's too many of them already done got killed behind this business."

The three men swapped confirming glances and it was Bean who answered for them. "We c'n do that, Bass. Where you going?"

"Got to go get my warrants and my guns. Then I'll be back. Could I trouble one a'you gentlemen to go around the front of The Baker House and get my horse? He's tied up in front."

"I'll do it," Dave Massey said and departed on that errand.

"And just what are we supposed to do if you can't arrest Joe and Ricky, Reeves?" Mitchum wanted to know. "We'll be in just as bad a fix as we were before you came."

"Then I guess you'll just have to go to Fort Smith and get that twelve man posse," Bass answered with a smile.

"I don't think that's funny!"

"Believe it or not, neither do I."

Ricky Chance burst into The Black Horseshoe, his eyes wild. He ran over to where his brother sat and said, "Did you take that nigra outta the cell?"

Joe poured himself a drink. "No. Why would I do that? What ails you?"

"He's gone!"

"Gone? What do you mean, gone?"

"I mean he's gone! Just like he disappeared!"

"That's impossible. He'd have to get through two locked doors to get out."

"Well, he done it. I don't know how. I went back to the office, unlocked the outer door, walked back to the cells to check on him and he was gone. And his cell door was still locked as well."

Joe stood up and headed for the batwing doors of the saloon. "You haven't seen Claude nor Bob? Maybe they come back and took him out?"

"In that case, why would they lock everything back up behind them? And you know full well that they wouldn't have taken him out without gettin' the say-so from you, Joe."

And Joe did know that. He was just hoping against hope that this time he'd be wrong. Not that he blamed his brothers for letting the prisoner escape. He blamed himself. His instincts had practically screamed at him that there was something not right about Butterfield and he hadn't listened.

Once back inside the Sheriff's office, Joe performed a quick search. The back door was locked as well so Butterfield hadn't gone out that way. And yes, the cell door had been securely locked.

"How you figure he got out, Joe? You reckon he could be a conjure man?"

"Don't talk stupid. Either somebody let him out or he had a key on him. I shoulda searched him. Dammit!" Joe snatched his hat off and whacked his leg with it. That was two mistakes in one day. Time to slow down, take stock and start thinking because Joe had the unpleasant feeling that if he made a third mistake today, that would be the mistake that would get him killed.

Ricky's next words snatched him out of his reverie; "Some kinda hullabaloo outside, Joe."

Joe pushed Ricky aside in his haste to get to the door he opened it to see several of the town's professional loafers holding onto the reins of two horses. Horses that Joe identified immediately as belonging to his brothers.

"Found these horses just moseying back into town, Sheriff," one of the loafers said. "I know this one belongs to Claude so I'm figuring that t'other is Bob's."

The townspeople that had gathered around murmured to themselves and Joe didn't like the sound of that at all. "Y'all go on about your business. Go on, git!"

"Where are your brothers, Sheriff? You don't suppose something happened to them, did you?" The gentleman who said that had a huge grin of pleasure on his face. Obviously the thought that something amiss might have befallen Claude and Bob delighted him to no end.

He went to the other side with that smile on his face because Joe shot him right in the forehead. "When I say git, I mean git!" Joe roared, firing two more shots in the air. Within ten seconds the crowd dispersed with only dust trails to signify they had been there at all. Nobody bothered to take the body with them.

"Where's Claude and Bob, Joe? Why did their horses come back without them?"

"Don't be a damn fool, Ricky. You know why. Get them horses round to the back outta sight. I'm going to get Greta. We gotta plan our next move real careful."

"What about that nigra?"

"The hell with him! Ain't you figured out yet that he's in with whoever got Claude and Joe? The two of them is most likely dead by now!"

Ricky blinked, obviously hurt by the very thought. "Maybe they just been captured," he said in a low, hollow voice.

"After all we done in this town and the others we got hired on in, would you let yourself be taken alive by the law?"

"No. I wouldn't."

"So why would Claude and Bob be any different? They're dead alright. Now go do what I told you!"

Bass rode up to the dry wash. Tom Lucky had recovered the wagon from its place of concealment and Bass could see Claude and Bob Chance securely locked up in the cage. Claude glared hate. Bob lay stretched out. Sonny Calvera stood next to the cage and turned to greet Bass with a wave as he rode up. "What ails Bob?" Bass wanted to know.

"Nothing now," Sonny said. "Damn fool wouldn't surrender. Had no choice."

"Hey! Hey you! Nigger! Yeah, I'm talking to you!" Claude yelled. "Who are you? What give you and these bushwhackin' bastards the right to gun down duly appointed Sheriffs?"

"I'll be more than happy to show you the warrants I got for the arrest of you, your brothers and your sister, Claude. I'm U.S. Deputy Marshal Bass Reeves and I aim to see you and the rest of your kin hang for multiple counts of murder, mayhem and malfeasance perpetrated against the law abidin' citizens of the town of Affliction. Especially your brother Joe. Because he was a lawman down in Texas and he knows better."

Claude's eyes plainly showed his surprise at this new intelligence. "Bass Reeves. I heard a'you."

"And I have most certainly heard'a you and your kin. Man name of

*"When I say git, I mean git!"*

Baker got the good folks of Affliction to swear out complaints against ya'll. You killed him for it and you tried to kill Deputy Marshal Corky Burress. We can't have that sort of thing going on in this here territory. Next thing you know, all sorts of no-counts will think they can shoot up Deputy Marshals and get away with it." Bass climbed down from the horse. "Tom, fix me up a plate. Think I'll let Joe and Ricky stew awhile in their own juices before I go back into town."

"How long are we going to just sit here?" Greta Chance demanded. A tall, muscular woman with straight chocolate hair and almond-shaped grey eyes she looked as if she belonged on the great stages of famous international theaters. She carried herself with the grace and haughtiness of royalty. This was all part of her carefully cultivated image. Greta Chance was every inch as dangerous as her brothers. Even more so, in fact as men were wont to let their guard down around her due to her manner and her beauty. Plenty of those same men had died at her hands.

Ricky sat behind the bigger desk where he had passed the time cleaning his guns. "Joe said for the two of us to stay here until he says different and that's just want we're gonna do. So stop your complaining. This situation is bad enough without me having to listen to your whinin'."

"If it's that bad then we need to pull up stakes and light out of here! We've got pretty near twenty thousand in the safe at my cathouse! That's more than enough to get us back to Texas and the rest of the money we've got laid away down there! The law here won't send anybody down to Texas after us!"

"You want to get caught out there on the trail with who knows how big a posse they got? They could have fifty men out there just waiting' to gun us down as we ride outta town."

"If they had a posse that big then why don't they just ride into town and take us? What are they waiting for?"

Ricky stopped his cleaning long enough to glare at his sister. He never did like how she could out-talk him. "Look, Joe said for us to stay here and wait and that's good enough for me. And that means it's good enough for you as well. Joe runs the show and what he says, goes." Ricky furiously resumed cleaning his gun.

Greta gave out with that feminine specific 'harrumph' that contained an entire dictionary full of meaning. Ricky didn't care as long as she did what she was told.

"Joe is sure that Claude and Bob are dead, then?"

"He's pretty sure. He says that Claude and Bob wouldn't let themselves be taken alive."

"And how about you?"

Ricky again stopped his cleaning and looked at his sister with confused suspicion. "What do you mean?"

"I mean when the Marshals and their fifty man posse ride on in here are you going to let them take you alive or are you going to get gunned down like Claude and Bob?" Greta wished mightily that Bob had been left here with her instead of Ricky. Bob would have gone along with whatever she said without thinking twice. She and Bob would have been halfway to Texas by now.

"If you're 'bout to suggest what I think your 'bout to suggest then you can stop right there, Greta. I don't want to hear any more."

"Just give me two minutes, Ricky. Hear me out." Greta stood up and crossed the room with a rustling of her skirts. She leaned on the desk and spoke in a low, urgent voice; "You said that Joe is sure that Claude and Bob are dead. If that's so then we can't be of any help to them and there sure isn't any point in us hanging around, then. Joe can look after himself. He used to be a lawman. He's still got friends down in Texas who have weight enough to see that he won't hang. Oh, sure, he'll have to do time in prison. But he'll be alive! That leaves us. Who do we have to look out after us? Nobody!"

"Joe will look out after us!"

"Joe will have a hard enough time making sure that he doesn't hang! After he calls in all his favors to keep his neck out of the noose do you think he'll have any left over for us? Hell, no! And I'm not sticking around to take that chance! I'm going to get that money and I'm hightailing it out of here! I'm going back to Texas and you can come with me if you want."

Ricky reassembled his guns while Greta spoke. He reloaded them slowly and deliberately. "Now I see why Joe wanted me to stay and keep an eye on you. You'd have taken the money and left long before this, wouldn't you?"

"All I'm saying is that there really isn't any point to the both us staying and getting killed now is there? Why don't you think for yourself for a change and stop licking Joe's boots?"

Ricky jumped up, pushing his chair back. "Don't you go talkin' about Joe like that! He's our brother! We're family and we stick together, no matter what!"

"Joe isn't here! He's busy pickling his brains while you're sitting here waiting to get killed by that posse!"

"Joseph Alan Chance! Richard Chance! This is U.S. Deputy Marshal Bass Reeves! I have legal warrants issued by the Honorable Judge Isaac Parker of the United States Court for the Western District of Arkansas for your arrest! I hereby direct you to come out unarmed and with your hands up! Ignore my directive at your peril!"

Ricky and Greta looked at each other with wide open eyes for about ten seconds. Ricky said, "You slip out the back way and go warn Joe while I take care of this."

He didn't have to tell Greta twice. She was gone while the last syllable of his last words still vibrated in the air. Ricky adjusted his gun belt, walked over to the door. Opened it and stepped out onto the sidewalk.

Bass Reeves stood there in the street, a breeze billowing his ankle-length duster. He had changed back into his regular clothes and his star shone proudly on the lapel of his vest.

Ricky chuckled. "Now don't you look all purty. Gone and got yourself cleaned up now did you?"

"That I did. How you figure on playin' this out, Ricky?"

"My name is Mr. Chance, boy. Just 'cause you dress like a white man don't make you one, hear?"

Bass held up a piece of paper. "This here is your warrant, Ricky. Once you're shackled you can look it over."

"Where are my brothers?"

"Claude's still alive. He's smart. Bob's dead. He wasn't smart."

Ricky's young face tightened with hatred. "You black son of a bitch," he snarled as his hands hovered above his guns.

"Don't. You and your kin had a pretty good run but it's over. Time to pay the fiddler for the dance."

Ricky's hands blurred toward his guns. Bass let go of the warrant and his right hand went to his. The sounds of three gunshots exploded in the humid air, fading away even as the warrant hit the ground, raising a tiny puff of dust. Ricky twisted as if he'd suddenly got a cramp in his stomach. He stumbled backwards; hit the door of the Sheriff's office. He brought up his guns again, tried to fire. Bass shot him again. Ricky hit the sidewalk, rolled into the street, his guns flying from his hands. Bass bent down to pick up the warrant. He folded it carefully, put it back in his vest pocket then headed toward the Black Horseshoe. The townspeople came out of their hiding places now. Some ran toward Ricky's body. Others looked at Bass in open fear or total surprise.

Bass paused for a bit at the batwing doors of the Black Horseshoe. Joe would have the advantage since it would take a few seconds for Bass' eyes to adjust to the dim interior of the saloon. But Bass reckoned he wouldn't have to worry about that. He pushed open the doors and went on in.

Joe sat at his favorite table. Bottle within reach, glass in hand. His gun lay in the table. Joe grinned easily, as if Bass were an old friend he had been expecting to join him. "Bass Reeves. I shoulda guessed it was you right from the start. Back in my office when you positioned yourself the way you did, my belly did a backflip. But I didn't listen to it."

"Got a warrant here for your arrest, Joe. For your brothers and sister as well."

"Judging by the gunshots I heard you tried to serve Ricky his. Lemme guess; Ricky's dead."

"So is Bob. You, Claude and Greta are still alive. You can keep it that way."

"If I know Greta, she's vamoosed. Cleaned out her safe and is on her way back to Texas."

"She won't get far. I got a posseman waiting for her at her cathouse. He's got her in custody by now."

Joe chuckled, poured himself a drink. "I'd be pleased and proud if'n you join me for a drink."

The wrist shackles Bass threw landed on the table next to the bottle. The patrons of the saloon slowly and furtively made their way toward the door. The bartender calmly poured himself a drink and watched. No way in hell was he going to miss this. This was a story he could tell for years to customers who would empty their pockets for drink after drink while the bartender spun his yarn.

"Put 'em on, Joe and let's go."

"No reason to be rude about this, Bass."

"You don't deserve politeness, Joe. You were an honored and respected lawman down in Texas. Ain't nothing worse than a lawman goes back on his oath and turns outlaw. And you used the law to rob honest, hard-workin' folks."

Joe shrugged. "What can I say? Them's the one with the money."

"What happened to you, Joe?"

Joe Chance shrugged again. "One day I looked around and saw everybody else was getting' richer than me and living better than me and all I was doing was stayin' in the same spot. My life wasn't getting any better and all I was doing was capturing men to be killed or killin' them myself."

"So then you quit. You put down the badge and find yourself something else to do. Or if you want to rob and steal, have the backbone not to hide behind the law while you do it."

"Don't be so high and mighty with me, Bass. Hell, half the lawmen workin' this territory were outlaws themselves at one time or another. If'n I recall the stories I heard about you, you was supposed to have been a runaway slave. Killed your massa, I was told."

"My story ain't important right now, Joe. Yours is. Put them shackles on and let's go."

Joe chuckled again. "C'mon now, Bass. You knew full well from the start that there warn't but one way this was going to play out. You take me into Fort Smith alive in the morning and I'll hang before lunch. Judge Parker has got to make an example out of me. That ain't any way for me to go out."

"You want to do it here or out in the street?"

Joe took another drink. "Here is just a good a place as any." Joe stood up, picked up his gun and slid it into his holster. He stepped away from the table to give himself plenty of room.

"You ready?" Bass asked.

"Yep."

For perhaps thirty seconds both men stood as still as statues. Only their eyes moving. Eyes trained and honed by many years of gunfights, looking for that telltale gesture or unconscious flicker of the eyelids that would indicate that the other man was going for his firearm. Gunfights were lost and won on that fraction of a fraction of a second that gave a man the advantage on the draw and enabled him to get off a shot faster than his opponent.

Joe's hand moved at a speed it seemed impossible for a human being to achieve. The watching bartender blinked. He hadn't even seen Joe's hand move but suddenly, it held a gun. Two gunshots echoed in the saloon.

Joe grinned as he twirled his gun back into the holster. With careful, measured steps he walked back to the table and poured himself a drink in the shot glass. He carefully set the bottle back down. And then Joe Chance toppled over backwards to crash to the floor, raising a cloud of sawdust.

Bass walked over to the table, picked up the shot glass and threw back the drink. He looked down at the body of Joe Chance. His eyes were still open and Bass would have sworn right then and there that the eyes of Joe Chance now had more life and emotion in them than when he was alive.

The clanging of the cell door made Claude Chance wince. Plainly he was used to being on the other side of the door. "Where you put my sister, Reeves?"

"Judge Parker doesn't allow women to be kept down here in Hell on The Border. No matter what they done. He's got her someplace secure." Greta Chance was secure in the military guardhouse where female prisoners were housed until the disposition of their case.

Claude hawked and spit on the filthy floor of his cell. "It stinks in here!"

"You're lucky this ain't the summertime. I've seen men pass out from the smell on a hot July afternoon."

"This ain't right, Reeves! This just ain't right!"

"Tell that to the men you killed and the families you robbed in Affliction." Bass replied coldly. He turned and strode away, ignoring the curses and insults thrown at him by the other residents of Fort Smith Federal Prison. Many of them he'd put here and they awaited trial in front of Judge Parker. They'd be better off staying right where they were. Not for nothing was Judge Parker known as "The Hanging Judge."

Bass went on upstairs to the spacious courthouse and walked through it to Judge Parker's office and knocked respectfully on the door. "Come on in, Bass!"

Bass opened the door and went on in, taking off his hat. Judge Parker looked up from the paperwork strewn about on his desk and smiled. "Glad to see you, Bass. C'mon in and take a seat. Relax for a minute."

Bass did so, saying, "Never can figure out how you know my knock."

"I know all the knocks of my deputies. How a man knocks on a door is unique as the man himself. You got the Chances, I take it?"

Bass placed the warrants on Parker's desk. "Claude is downstairs and I took Miss Chance over to the military guardhouse. The others are dead. They wouldn't come peaceable like."

Parker sighed, picked up the warrants and shuffled through them. "I'd have preferred that they all be taken alive, especially Joe. But if you say they gave you no choice, that's good enough for me. You got a sizeable bounty coming to you, Bass. You want it now or you going to stay overnight in town with your boy?"

Bass cocked his head in surprise. "My boy? Which boy?"

"Robert. Way he told it, Corky Burress kicked up such a ruckus out at your place that the boy loaded him into a wagon and brought him here. Said he'd stay on until you came back. He's staying over to the Meachams."

Bass nodded. Carson Meacham was another Negro Deputy Marshal who lived in Fort Smith with his wife and three daughters. Bass himself had stayed there many a night himself.

"You can give me enough to pay off Tom and Sonny for their work. They done real good. I'll pick up the balance in the morning."

Judge Parker swiveled around in his chair and opened the waist-high Anderson & McGee safe. He withdrew a cashbox from within and placed it on his desk. He counted out the required amount Bass needed to pay his men and returned the cashbox to the safe. "I appreciate what you've done, Bass. The Chances gave us a black eye but you kicked their teeth out. Word gets around about this, owlhoots will think twice. I still wish you could have brought Joe Chance in alive."

Bass put the money in his pocket and replaced his hat on his head. "Nossir, Judge. I really don't think it would have served anything to hang Joe Chance. I looked in his eyes plenty before we drew iron. Joe Chance was dead. Dead for a long time before me and him met up. I just put him out of his misery is all." Bass touched the brim of his hat. "I'll be back in the morning for the rest of the money."

Bass left the office and strode back through the courtroom and out into the bustling streets of Fort Smith. He looked around for Tom Lucky and Sonny Calvera. More than likely they were somewhere getting properly liquored up.

"Pa!"

Bass turned to see Robert trotting across the half-muddy road. He stuck out his hand to shake his father's.

"Judge Parker said you brought Corky Burress into town. What happened?"

"Ah, he got to fussin' and complainin'. Said he needed to know what was going on and he just couldn't lay there doing nothing. I told Ma I'd bring him back here so he'd stop devilin' her."

Bass nodded. "'Preciate it, son. You got that Spanish Mustang broke?"

Robert grinned with pride, actually puffing out his chest a bit. "The same day you left, Pa. He's all gentle-like now."

Bass nodded. "C'mon, then." Bass walked back into the road, heading for the other side of the street.

"Where we going, Pa?"

"Thought I'd like to have a drink with my son at Miss Zenobia's. If'n you don't have anything else to do, that is?"

Robert's grin grew so wide it threatened to meet in the back of his head. "Naw, Pa. Don't have a thing I'd rather do."

Bass Reeves threw his arm around his son's shoulders and they navigated their way through the busy streets of Fort Smith. He enjoyed the feel of his son's strong shoulders under his arm, the sunlight on his face and the sounds and smells of life around him. He'd learned something in his encounter with Joe Chance and he hoped it was something he learned that would keep him on the path he'd chosen for his life.

THE END

# Who is Bass Reeves and Where Has He Been All My Life?

How is it that I have read so much (and seeing as how I'm comfortably in my 50s I have read a LOT, trust me) and never heard or read anything about Bass Reeves?

Seriously. It made me downright embarrassed when Ron Fortier and I met at the first Pulp Ark convention and during one of the numerous conversations we had that weekend he told me about Bass Reeves. He came out with dates and statistics and locations and all sorts of data that backed up the stories he related to me over the course of those three days. And when I got back home to Brooklyn I followed up, doing my own research to dig up even more details about this fabulous individual.

Wyatt Earp. Doc Holliday. Bat Masterson. Buffalo Bill. Charlie Siringo. Cole Younger. John Wesley Hardin. Wild Bill Hickok. These are names that we still remember and are renowned as legends of the Old West, the Wild West. Because their stories have been told and retold in novels, movies, comic books, radio dramas and TV shows until they've become integral threads in the great and grand tapestry of American Mythology.

But where is Bass Reeves in this tapestry? Where are his comic books? His radio dramas? His movies? His TV shows?

Hopefully this anthology will be the beginning of a Bass Reeves renaissance that will spread his legend far and wide. Ever since Ron told me about him, I've been making notes and stockpiling ideas, scenes and character profiles for a Bass Reeves novel (that I still intend to write, never fear) but I always said to Ron that if he ever decided to do a Bass Reeves anthology, I wanted in. Well, he did and therefore, I did. And among the many projects I've done, this one truly is special. I know, I know, you've heard that before from me and from other writers. But this one…it does mean a lot.

Part of the reason I got into this crazy writing biz is because growing up I read, enjoyed and loved the adventures of Tarzan, Doc Savage, The Lone Ranger and other pulp adventure characters. But there was something I noticed: there were no heroic black characters of similar stature. You gotta remember that I grew up during the 1970s which to a lot of you is a period of time as remote and alien as The Mesozoic Age. I couldn't Google a blessed thing like I can now to find out anything and everything I want.

But I did know as I got older and cemented my desire to be a writer until it became reality that I wanted to write the kind of books I wished had been there for me to read when I was a kid. And so that's why I created Dillon (my homage to Doc Savage) and soon you'll be reading about Voodah, a character that wasn't created by me but one that I saw could be my homage to Tarzan and other Lords of The Jungle. With the difference being that Voodah is black (you'll be hearing more about him later on, trust me).

And in Bass Reeves I saw a chance to bring an authentic black hero of the Old West to life. And what was even better was that I didn't have to make him up. He was REAL.

My greatest wish is that this will be just the first of many Bass Reeves anthologies to come and that the stories written by not only myself but the other outrageously talented writers who contributed will inspire others to learn more about the magnificent legend that is Bass Reeves and add to his legend.

**DERRICK FERGUSON** – is a native of Brooklyn, New York which as all right thinking people know is The Center of The Universe. He's lived there most of his still young life. He has been married for 30 years to the wonderful Patricia Cabbagestalk-Ferguson who lets him get away with far more than is good for him.

His interests include radio/audio drama, Classic Pulp from the 30's/40's/50's and New Pulp being written today, Marvel and DC superheroes, Star Trek in particular and all Science Fiction in general, animation, television, movies, cooking, loooooong road trips and casual gaming on the Xbox 360.

Books he has written include:
*Dillon and the Voice of Odin*
*Dillon and the Legend of the Golden Bell*
*Four Bullets For Dillon*
*Dillon And The Pirates of Xonira*
*Young Dillon In The Halls of Shamballah*
*The Vril Agenda (with Joshua Reynolds)*
*The Adventures of Fortune McCall*
*Fight Card: Brooklyn Beatdown (as Jack Tunney)*
All of which are available through Amazon.com as paperbacks and ebooks.

In addition he has stories in the following volumes:
*How The West Was Weird Vol. I*
*How The West Was Weird Vol.II*
*How The West Was Weird Vol. III*
*How The West Was Weird: Campfire Tales* (which is available only as an Ebook)
*Tales From The Hanging Monkey*
*Sinbad-The New Voyages*
All of which are available as paperbacks and ebooks from Amazon.com

For further information about Derrick Ferguson, what he's up to and what he's going to do next we invite you to check out at your convenience these sites:
Blood & Ink http://dlferguson-bloodandink.blogspot.com/
Dillon https://derrickferguson1.wordpress.com/
The Ferguson Theater http://derricklferguson.wordpress.com/

Made in the USA
Middletown, DE
28 September 2017